Sign up for our newsletter to hear
about new and upcoming releases.

www.ylva-publishing.com

OTHER BOOKS IN THE SUPERHEROINE COLLECTION

Shattered by Lee Winter
The Power of Mercy by Fiona Zedde
Chasing Stars by Alex K. Thorne
Shadow Hand by Sacchi Green

A LOVER'S MERCY

FIONA ZEDDE

CHAPTER 1

"I want you to meet my family," Mai says in the quiet of our bedroom.

Her dark-gold eyes are cautious, a pink-tinged lower lip caught between her teeth. The warm weight of her, draped over mine, feels almost too light.

She's nervous.

Because I'm not a complete ass, I bite back my automatic refusal. "Why? Do you want me to kill them, too?"

It's a bit of a sore spot between us that I murdered her uncle a few months ago.

A wince tics across her beautiful face, and she turns away to give me the curled C of her back. But it's only to reach for the water on the bedside table. She drinks and looks over her shoulder at me with her soul in her eyes. The thick cloud of hair around her face, an angel's corona, bounces with her movements and exhales the scent of rose-infused shea butter.

"Sometimes you can be cruel." Her look tells me she doesn't know whether or not she thinks that's a good thing.

"I know."

Mai returns the water glass to the table and settles herself next to me instead of on top as we both prefer. Iridescent scales ripple across her throat, a brief loss of control of her newly realized powers. Seconds later, the scales disappear into her skin like they were never there.

So beautiful.

I caress the line of skin, following its softness under the open collar of the pale yellow sleep shirt she wears.

My love is a chameleon and shape-shifter, who can change her body into whatever she pleases. She can give herself claws that shred, a long tail to pick up a glass from the countertop, a rippled tongue to fuck me until I scream.

Barely three months ago, Mai's long-dormant Meta powers came bursting to the surface. It was only then that her power-rich family started to pay more attention to her.

Mai sees through them. It's obvious why they're suddenly interested in her being a real part of the family, but knowing their motives doesn't make her want her family any less.

Although she's strong, they make her think she's weak.

Her back is delicate as steel under my hands. I trace its curve through the soft cotton of her shirt. "They don't deserve you and you know it. If you ever change your mind about me killing your mommy dearest, or any of them, I am completely at your service. One trained enforcer assassin to do whatever you want." My voice drops to a low purr. "Whenever you want." She can take that however she likes.

Rising up from her pillow, Mai squirms, delicious and conflicted. She's so sweet I could just drink her all up.

"No, thank you. I told you, I don't want them dead." A frown marks her forehead. With a hand hooked around the back of my neck and tangled in the ends of my short hair, she drags my mouth to hers. "You're so horrible," she says against my lips.

I know she doesn't mean it as foreplay but *Christ*, the way she says, it makes me ache.

"All this sweet talk will get you nowhere with me." Smiling and leaning close, I unbutton her sleep shirt, just to make sure she knows what direction my thoughts are heading. "I'm not going to your mother's house with you so you can just give that up right now." My hands drift down her clenching belly to the mound between her thighs. I grip her gently, teasing the delicate flesh. "And I'd dearly love for you to give this up, too."

A soft whine of protest leaves her lovely throat. "Stop trying to distract me." Her whine turns into a low moan from the movement of my fingers. "God, that feels so good…"

My mouth presses into hers and smothers her gasp. I play between her legs, distracting her from how much I love this sensuous mouth of hers. Kissing is a soft thing, not meant for people like me. With Mai, it's a guilty pleasure I can't get enough of.

Her lips are absolutely perfect. A more luscious shape, texture, or flavor has never existed, at least not as far as I'm concerned. When in my arms, she always smells of desire, the thick and salty aroma rising from between her legs like smoke from home fires. Even when she's angry with me.

But her lips… They call to me like the softness denied to me over the years of my life. Hard training with the enforcers left me merciless. When Mai's cousin killed my only sister, Ixchel, just a baby and mine to protect, I lost my mind for a few years and did things I should be ashamed of. And until very recently, all I had was my job as an enforcer and the games I played to get revenge on the monster who took her away from me.

Now though, I have Mai. And her incredible lips.

Soft and tender and loving. They welcome mine with a sigh, parting and tilting up to receive me. The top and bottom lips mirror each other, identical. I've stared at them and visually measured enough to be convinced of this. There's a small dimple just below them. Mai denies it exists, but it's true. When she's tired, it's there. When she just barely stops herself from confessing how much she loves me, it appears. A telltale sign of her feelings. I press my lips briefly to it.

"Stop playing with me." She gasps and moves impatiently against the bed.

My tongue flicks a line from her top to bottom lip, almost a dry stroke. Her breath hitches. Impatient fingers grab the edge of the oversized T-shirt I wear to bed and pull it off me, briefly interrupting our kiss.

"Hm. That's better." Mai strokes my naked back and lower, pulling me closer and demanding more. Her long body maneuvers its way under me, and she grips my short hair in a fist, intoxicatingly ready for a long night enclosed in the warmth of our bedroom with me.

My body melts. The breath trips in my throat.

It's incredible that this is the very same bed I trapped her against when I broke into her apartment a few months ago, intending to warn her from investigating the murders I committed. Now, this is the place where she welcomes me. Makes love to me. Challenges me to be better.

I'm nothing special. Powerful, yes, but Mai doesn't care about that. Without my power, I'm just an ordinary woman. Short, black curls in a pixie cut that shows off my pointed ears, a usefully slender body, and eyes that deceive. But she wants me just the same.

With my breathing not quite so steady, I pull back from her lips, but only a little. "What about the dinner with your family?" I ask. A shallow probe at her slick entrance provokes a moan, and I laugh softly, the wickedness she likes in me coming out to play. "Don't you want to talk more about it?" A little deeper and she cries out, digging her fingers into my back.

"Xóchitl, are—are you trying to drive me out of my m-mind?"

"Never. I want you sane and with me for a very long time to come." But I move my fingers inside her again, kissing her incredible lips, savoring the pleasure that her pleasure brings me.

The sound of her passion rings through the room, loud and heady, and I feel her beginning to fumble between my thighs, but I pull her hand away and trap it above her head. That's not what I want right now.

"I need more. Xóchitl, please..." How she begs me. The way she calls my name. Doesn't try to shorten it to something her American tongue is already used to. This is an aphrodisiac in itself.

"More of what, Mai?" My fingers tease her shallowly.

"Just fuck me already!"

4

Her profanity makes me laugh. Chuckling into the thickness of her hair, I gladly give her what she wants. The liquid drive of my fingers inside her wanting center wrings a cry from us both.

A low sound bursts out into the room. Her telephone.

Beneath me, Mai stiffens. Her eyes fly open and she moans for an entirely different reason. "No, no, no…" But her hips keep moving, thrusting up to greedily take everything I give her. That moment of self-indulgence doesn't last long. Growling in frustration, she pushes my hands away from between her thighs then dives across the bed to grab the cell phone.

"Mercy," she answers with barely a tremor in her voice.

Fighting back a curse, I roll onto my back and drop a hand over my eyes. Now that we're not kissing, I become aware of just how turned on I am. My thighs are soaked and the most urgent of tingles vibrate in my belly. If we'd kept going for any longer, my orgasm would've snuck up on me. Nothing I'd complain about, obviously.

But damn human cops.

"I hope I wasn't interrupting anything," a male voice says through the phone. It's not loud but my hearing easily catches everything he's saying.

"You actually are," I mutter, making no effort to keep my voice down.

The imbecile doesn't hear me. Mai gives me a shushing glance to which I only reply with a widening of my thighs to show her how desperately aroused I am. She bites her lip and turns away.

"Don't worry about it," she says into the phone. "What can I do for you?"

"I know you haven't heard from us in a while, but this current situation requires your particular skills." The idiot on the other end of the line sounds satisfied with himself. Like he's doling out compliments to someone starved for them. Maybe he is.

"Tell me more." She climbs out of the bed, already in superhero mode.

While I vaguely entertain the thought of taking care of my own orgasm while she's on the phone, the whole sad story comes pouring

5

out. Apparently, there's a hostage situation. A group of criminals broke into a politician's house and have his entire family prisoner. Husband, kids, dog, everything. This politician is unexpectedly away at some sort of impromptu meeting, which is a happy coincidence for him.

The criminals have lots of guns and demands only the politician can fulfill. Some strange kind of political blackmail. Do those humans think they can actually get away with this?

The cop finishes up by asking, "Can you help?"

"Of course." Mai doesn't hesitate. "Where is all this happening?"

He quickly gives her the address and gets her agreement to be there in return before he ends the call.

"Why do I get the feeling I'm about to get left high and wet?" I watch as she shrugs off what little clothes she has on.

Already in mid-change, her soft skin transforming into hard, burgundy leather—a true transformation this time instead of the mere illusions she was capable in the past—Mai turns to frown at me. "We're not done talking about this."

"Talking about what? You abandoning your girlfriend's very urgent sexual needs to go play with a bunch of humans in uniform?"

A balled-up shirt narrowly misses my face. But only because I catch it mid-air.

"No—dinner with my family. Don't pretend like you don't know what I'm talking about."

"Well, darling, your sweet lips made me forget everything but the way you taste. Can you blame me?"

"Yes, I actually can." Fully changed, she is Mercy now. She wears skin-tight, dark red leather, complete with a mask only showing her intense and long-lashed eyes. It looks like she's been skiing in blood. The wet place between my thighs gives a hard and powerful throb.

All I want to do is wrestle her to bed and make love to her until she forgets she even got a phone call. Those cops of hers wouldn't see her for days. To hell with the stupid politician who can't keep his own family safe.

But I can't do that.

"See you right here when you get back," I murmur with an airy wave. The silk sheets shift under me as I adjust myself against the pillows, and a hint of moonlight pours through the window to fall like liquid silver over my naked breasts. Mai stares because she can't help herself. "Be safe while you're out there saving the world." I hide my smile when she tears her eyes away from me with visible effort.

"Right. Okay." A shiver runs through her body. Then she shakes her head, the tiniest of smiles shaping her mouth. "Why are you such a terrible person?"

"Because you wouldn't want me any other way?"

A sound of exasperation leaves her lips, then she is at the bedroom's wide window, sliding it open. "I'll be back before you fall asleep." She slips out into the night.

I take a breath. Then two.

With Mai gone, the apartment is quiet. Just the sounds of the various appliances carrying on with their business. The quiet hum of the central air conditioning. The fridge that never has enough food for her, let alone the two of us. The computer she left on after she finished grading papers for the night.

A few more breaths pass while I lay in bed, watching the empty window and listening to Mai's quiet steps along the side of the building, then up to the roof. She's gone to save the world while I lay here, saving nothing. My chance at making a change, at saving something precious, came and went with my sister, Ixchel. She died alone, in terror.

And I became...this.

Usually, I allow introspection to pass me by, but there's something about this moment. It feels like nighttime crept into the room with me as Mai crept out, bringing with it its shadows that mirror mine.

I have too many secrets to count. They've accumulated like dirt under fingernails while grasping in desperation at a life lived on the surface of violence. That's why I like Mai Redstone so much. This foolish, beautiful creature with a family of vipers and a heart big enough for all of Atlanta to live in. She's as naked to me as a newborn sliding from their mother's bloodied crease, and that makes me cherish her even more. That's what makes me want to keep her safe.

And that's the only reason I can think of why I get up from the nest of comfortable silk sheets, get dressed, and follow the path she took out of the apartment and into the night. She's too important for me to lose her now.

CHAPTER 2

THE POLITICIAN LIVES IN A nice part of town. Wide streets. A coffee shop on every corner. Dog groomers and mayonnaise shops all over the place. But that didn't stop the guys with guns from breaking in and demanding whatever it is that these types always seem to want. The police officer on the phone seemed to think it's more than that. Of course, he would know more about human motivations than me.

So would Mai, actually.

Following her is as easy as it's always been. She may be able to change her shape and camouflage her body to blend into the surroundings, but she's always visible to me now. Easily found.

The reason for it is part of my power, which is why the enforcers came knocking on my mother's door when I was a child. Each Meta sends out a particular kind of energy on the spectrum I'm able to see. Not only is my power strong, it's also one that few Metas can protect themselves against. Although Mai thinks I can read every mind I encounter, my power is not that. Not with other Metas who I can only sense but never read, unless I pull them into my heart and love them more than myself.

The way I love Mai.

All human minds, though, are completely transparent to me. Not necessarily their motives but their every thought is laid open for me to read and to see—if I'm interested enough to take a look. Living among humans and having that kind of ability would be agony if I weren't able to control it. But I can, and I do. Most times, I don't care enough what's going on in a human's mind to bother looking.

My thoughts about what I can and can't do slip away when Mai arrives at the house.

Oh. The humans have a lot of guns.

From high in a tall tree, I take in all the action in the two-story family home a few hundred yards away. I can see why the cops called Mai. This is what they'd call a lose-lose situation. Six humans with very large guns hold hostage the oversized cottage of a pair of four-year-old twins, a tiny beige dog, and a very pissed-off spouse.

The husband is big. He either lifts weights or injects growth hormones in his spare time. In an ideal situation (for him), he could've taken out one or two of those guys in the house by himself. But as it is, there are six men of various sizes. Not to mention if he so much as twitches any of those large muscles the wrong way, I have no doubt the hostage takers would happily mow down one of the girls to teach him a lesson.

Two of the armed men have their semi-automatic weapons trained on the wide-eyed children and obliviously playful dog while another set threatens the husband, demanding to know where his other half is. The conversation sounds like it's on its third or fourth go-round. One of the men is on the phone, apparently trying to reach the politician husband. No obvious police cars lurk in the area. The confrontation looks very private.

With barely any effort, I sweep their minds, slipping in to rifle through their thoughts.

Oh, so the cop was right. This isn't a matter of a simple smash and grab: They want the politician to withhold his vote on something that matters to a lot of people in the city but means more to the corporations paying them. Didn't they stop doing this kind of obvious intimidation in the thirties?

Where is the man's husband, anyway?

Not that I actually care about where he is. The only person I care about is just about to do something stupid. Or, in her mind, "heroic." She's already talked to the people in charge. There's some kind of plan in place.

I hear her heartbeat. Her thoughts are focused. Through her eyes, I see everything: The house she crouches on top of. The cops waiting in darkness to do their part of the rescue mission. Her hands flex as power for her change floods her body with adrenaline that is like pain and pleasure both.

Now.

In a shower of multicolored glass, Mai bursts through the skylight with a snarl on her face and claws where fingers were moments before. Pieces of glass glitter around her as she lands in a crouch in front of the children, pulls them both to her, and throws her arms around them.

Not the safest approach.

With a rush of air, bat-like wings spring along her long arms and up her sides. The wings are a deep red and leatherlike, a match to her new skin, and are harder than steel. Without looking into her mind, I know she hasn't tested them before, not against bullets. Stupid woman.

Fear for her grips my throat tight.

With this terror pushing me on, I'm out of the tree and leaping onto the front porch when I hear the bullets spit from the guns, aimed right at Mai and the children. Semi-automatic weapons. Armor-piercing rounds. My heart nearly stops.

But the bullets bounce right off her skin like they're made of rubber and shower around the room, some flying back into the idiots who fired them in the first place. Mai grunts in satisfaction, whirls around still with the children in her arms, lifts them, even heavy as they are, and sprints toward an adjoining room.

As quickly as I got to the porch, I draw back, hiding again. Easily climbing up the roof, I crouch low to watch Mai's rescue come together.

Mai's appearance and very impressive distraction give the cops lurking at the back door just enough of an opening to burst in. Five officers, all in black, with their guns out, shout for the men to surrender or die. Their radios are squawking with all kinds of chatter as they swarm the gunmen, armed with their shields, bulletproof vests, and pistols. Not bad. But Meta enforcers could have done much better. When we go in, we are silent as death, and with a threat like this, we leave death in our wake as well.

None of these fools with guns would've survived to lie about who sent them. A roar breaks through the other noises in the house. The husband.

"You assholes!" With the police there and the criminals distracted, he rises up, a volcanic mountain spitting fire, and rushes toward one of his armed attackers. One of the men spins with his gun ready and fires blindly, eyes narrowed with anger and adrenaline at the sudden futility of his position. Oh, it's a woman. *Her* position, then.

She's bad enough at desperation to miss that massive target and hits the floor with a grunt, with a giant on top of her intent on murder.

"You tried to kill my kids, I'm going to fucking *murder* you!"

Gloved hands drag him off the woman before he can do more than shake her. "Who put you up to this?" Muscle Husband screams. "Who's doing this to us?" Then he suddenly remembers something more important. "Where are my girls? Where are the kids?"

The cops try to subdue him, and I'm impressed by how much effort it takes. Hopefully, the politician knows how lucky he is to have a partner like this. Or unlucky, if he's the one behind this foolish move.

Damn, why do I even care about this? Mai is the reason why I'm here, not to be amused by these people and their petty politics.

To be fair, Meta politics isn't too far removed from this. Only usually with more dead bodies and none of it ending up on the news.

Okay, enough. Mai is somewhere around here. Ah, there she is.

Safe. She hasn't done anything more stupid than usual. Breath flows easily through my body, and although I'm fairly certain nothing else will happen tonight, I don't lower my guard.

In the dark, where no one can see, she heads toward her human cops. She has both girls in her arms, one on each hip. Her bat wings are gone. Her face is still masked, but she's done something to it that makes her seem less frightening somehow. With a tenderness that's completely like her, she hands over the girls to two of the human police she works with in secret. The girls are sobbing, tears striping their faces as they call for their father.

Mai cups the cheek of each girl, one after the other, and leans in to say something to them. Miraculously, whatever she says works. They stop sobbing and fall into hiccups, staring at her with wide eyes and nodding like she's Disneyland opened up to them all at once.

I don't care enough to eavesdrop on the conversation. Her body is whole and unharmed. No bullets pierced her precious skin. No knife slashed into her stubborn hide. That's enough for me.

With her new and stronger abilities, Mai thinks she's nearly indestructible, but I know better than anyone how far from the truth that is. But she's mine to protect, whether she knows about it or not, whether she likes it or not. A smile from Mai, and the girls both lean in to try and fall into her arms again. But she stills them both and tips her head toward the house where Muscle Papa is having a coronary about his missing children.

The girls need to go back into the arms of the one they love. And Mai does, too.

I watch while she finishes up with her police. Lurking, listening. Making sure the way she moves isn't hiding an injury she doesn't want anyone to notice.

"Time for me to go back home," she tells the detective with the scar above his eye and a look on his face that says he'd love to see her off the clock sometime.

He's not even worth the effort of being jealous.

"Well, thank you for coming out on such notice. I know this isn't your usual thing—"

"My only usual thing is just helping people who aren't able to help themselves. I'm glad I could be of assistance."

It looks like he's going to say something else, but Mai's attention is already elsewhere, wondering if I'm already asleep and if I am, how mad will I be if she wakes me up. The need on her face makes me want to be very awake when she gets back to the condo.

"All right, take care of yourself now." He's obviously not taking his own advice since he allows his gaze to roam over Mai's body. It's a quick look, one she doesn't catch.

"All right, until next time." Already, she's walking away, her skin automatically changing to blend into the shadows.

That's my cue to leave.

The roof tiles hold firm under my boots as I climb down, then silently drop to the ground two floors below to follow and then pass Mai on her path back home. If I'm lucky, the adrenaline will still be flowing hot and strong through her when she gets into the apartment, powerful enough to drain her reason and memory.

If.

If that's the case, then she'll want me as soon as she climbs back through the window, her skin aching for hard contact and the exhaustion a few hours of rough love-making can bring. Only then will she allow me to distract her some more from that ridiculous dinner with her family that will never happen. Ever.

CHAPTER 3

"I TOLD THEM I'M SEEING someone." Mai nibbles on the edge of a wheat biscuit, ignoring the crumbs that drop into her lap and all over her white linen pants. Why my woman chose to wear white to a breakfast picnic in the park, I have no idea.

The sun blazes cool and gold over our morning picnic. A crisp October 10 a.m. with biscuits, red-pepper jelly, sausage made from spa-massaged turkeys, and gourmet coffee. My gift to her. Well, maybe it's a gift to both of us. Mai sometimes pretends she has no patience for romance, but I've seen into her dreams.

"You're an adult who also happens to like sex," I say from my place propped up against a pillow and on top of the thick blanket protecting us from the grass and its creepy-crawlies. "I hope that didn't surprise any of them." And by 'them,' I mean her mother.

Mai ignores my usual snark. "They want to know if you're human or Meta or…whatever."

Something about the way she's not looking my way makes me suspicious. I pause with the cup of coffee halfway to my mouth. "But you didn't tell them, did you?" My love is trying to keep secrets from her family, and it's kind of adorable. "You're hiding that I'm a Meta from them." Unlike most Metas, I can disguise who I am. It's part of my ability to hunt that the enforcers find useful.

"They don't have to know every little thing about me," Mai says, defensive.

The hot coffee floods over my tongue when I sip. Potent caffeine. Dark roasted and scalding. I swallow, then put aside the cup to stand on its own in the grass. "So you're just going to pretend they don't have eyes on just about everything you do?" Her family probably knows when we had sex for the first time. Not that our public parking lot sexcapade was that hard to miss, or catch on camera, by anyone passing by.

"They may be watching me but that doesn't mean they're in every part of my life." Her words are flippant, but the pain behind them squeezes my insides in a fist. Mai may have pulled away from her poisonous family to save herself, but she still loves them. Still wants those reptiles in her life.

The last of the biscuit disappears between her teeth in a final rain of crumbs. "Not the way I want them to be, at least." She looks wistful but angry with herself, too.

With my fingers linked with hers, I tug her down to the blanket with me. The autumn day is cool. Dying leaves fall from the tall trees and drift all around us. I lay back on the pillow with Mai draped over me and pull another thick blanket over us. The coolness of the day doesn't bother me, but there's something indescribably good about the intimacy of being under the covers together, even if it's in the middle of a city park.

Light as feathers, her bare toes brush back and forth over the top of my feet. "I'm sorry. I know you didn't plan this entire wonderful morning just for me to talk endlessly about my family." Her butter-scented breath brushes over my lips, and she rolls her eyes.

"I planned this so you can talk about whatever you want and to do whatever you want." As always, I can't keep my hands to myself. They wander over the curve of her hip and down to her thigh. "I won't lie and say I'm not tired of the subject though."

"Ha! I can always count on you to be honest with me, Xóchitl." She slides off me to land gently on her back but with her arm pressed against mine. Pushing away the blankets, she leaves herself bare to the chilled morning. Mai blinks up at the sky, smiling.

"I try to be honest with you, unless I can't." I carefully watch her face for the answer to my question. "Do you want me to start lying to you?"

"No, no! Please don't. I rely on you for that. Don't let my grouchiness convince you otherwise."

Her lips dip down at the corners, the smile quietly dying. I give in to the ever-present urge to kiss her. Lightly this time. A tease for now and a promise to get more later. "Grouchy doesn't suit you." This sadness popping up like a jack-in-the-box at unexpected moments has got to go, and for good. "That's more my MO."

I may be a bit of an ass, but part of what makes me so good at my real job is that I'm a natural protector. Sheltering the people I love from the things that hurt them, no matter how small, gives my life purpose. My mind skitters away from my little sister and just how much I failed to keep her safe.

"I don't think you're so much grouchy as have no time for anyone's shit," Mai says. "Even mine."

Instead of answering, I brush the soft line of her throat with my lips. The motion is so delicate that it tickles. She laughs again, trying to hide her vulnerable skin from me. I stop teasing before she can really get too far with that.

"Come on, eat some more." I steal one last kiss. "Your sister is going to drag you all over that museum, and you won't have time to eat before."

"I already ate half the food in that basket!"

I dip into the basket and produce a crisp slice of pear. "Eat the other half." A hum of satisfaction vibrates my chest when her lips part to accept the fruit. "You get any skinnier and I'll have to find a new girlfriend. You know I prefer my women thick and juicy."

"You ass!" She laughs, covering her mouth to stop pieces of chewed pear from flying everywhere.

"Don't worry, you're still juicy, so you still have that at least going for you." A piece of pear disappears into my mouth and I slowly chew, enjoying the strange mix of fruit and coffee on my tongue. Hm. What would pear-flavored coffee taste like? Hell, Starbucks will probably have that flavor next year as a special summer blend.

I love it when she laughs. When that smile of hers comes out, it pops instant gladness inside my chest. My happy by proxy. And in return for gifting me with some of the best days I've had so far, I want to give Mai Redstone everything.

I'm such a sap about Mai most days that I make myself sick.

Moments later, a butterfly lands on the back of her hand in a flutter of gold-dusted wings.

"Wow! Look!" Her thick lashes quiver in surprise, but other than that she stays perfectly still. "Xóchitl…isn't it beautiful?" Her voice comes out in a whisper like she's afraid that speaking too loudly will make the butterfly rush away. But it's not going anywhere. I've made sure of it.

The butterfly is a pretty thing. Its wings are like gauze. They wave back and forth through the air, filtering sunlight over Mai's skin. She stretches out her fingers to get a better look at the pretty creature on the back of her hand. Just then, another lands on her pinkie, then another on her arm. A gold-and-black monarch butterfly makes a landing strip of her shoulder. A heartbeat later, nearly a dozen of them, tiny and as white as her ridiculous pants, drift from a nearby tree and settle on her chest.

Mai's smile grows wider, and she stares at the butterflies using her as a perch like they are pure magic. More and more of them arrive. They flit across her skin, across her clothes, passing each other, but coming back to land on her like she's the most perfect flower they've found in the park.

Her eyes dart up to look me. "How are you not—Oh! You're doing this."

"Doing what, Mai darling?" But I'm smiling, and a dozen more butterflies flutter over to our blanket, landing in her hair, on her nose, on her smiling cheek.

They're in different patterns and colors: blue, green, yellow, a silken black with dots on its wings that look like eyes. I hear a gasp of surprise—someone passing by our mostly secluded spot. Then low conversations that sounds like strangers talking. But since it doesn't seem like anything dangerous, I only have eyes for Mai.

Soon, she's covered in butterflies, only with room to breathe and giggle about their tiny feet tickling her. Before her amazement can turn into a panic that she's covered in dozens of glorified bugs, I release the butterflies with a thought.

Like a rippling ribbon made up of a hundred colors, they rise from her skin, wings fluttering. They float up and up, undulating briefly above Mai like a flock of tiny birds, moving in a semi-solid mass, back and forth, showing off, before scattering in different directions.

Soon, it's just us and the bright blue sky and Mai's gentle amazement.

"That was a little incredible, and a lot sexy." She crouches over me, fingers clutching the loose fold of my cream-colored dress. "I'm saying this as someone who's seen some amazing things. You basically just guaranteed you'll be getting some tonight."

"I was already guaranteed a piece before all this," I tell her with a smug smile.

Although I've been semi-paying attention, I become aware of more eyes on us. Then a cell phone camera or five. The lenses of the phones are turned up toward the sky now and away from us. The few who'd been watching the butterfly show have already wandered away.

An annoyance. Why couldn't I have the power to harness lightning so I can fry these intrusive phones?

But then Mai presses me down into the blanket with more-than-PG-13 kisses, her mouth open and ravenous. It takes no more than that to make me forget all about the people watching us. My senses scatter like a thousand enchanted butterflies.

When she lifts her head a long time later, her lips are damp and swollen and her eyelids heavy from thoughts of sex. I brush my thumb along her lush lower lip and allow her thoughts to tug me along to that sweet and hot place. I squirm against the blanket. At least we don't have anything important to do later. We can take this picnic back to the bedroom and keep it going for the rest of the day and into the night.

What I want to eat right now I can't in public.

"So." She brushes her lips along my jaw. "What else can you do? You've never really told me."

Without my permission, my head tilts back, allowing Mai access to whatever part of me she wants. Traitorous body.

"Ah…" I swallow hard and dig my fingers into her hair when she finds that spot between my collarbones. She ghosts her tongue lightly over it, which basically acts like the key to opening my legs. I smell myself and I know she does, too.

My tongue tries to wipe away the dryness of my lips. "I'm a woman of many talents." A low moan breaks my reply in two. "I can't give away all my secrets to you so soon."

"Hm. So your powers are secret." Her gaze meets mine as she continues to tease.

From the spark in her eyes, I know she's joking. Mai doesn't want to measure my power and use that as a way to judge my worth. That's something her mother does. But she's also right that the things I can do are more secret than they are known.

The enforcers are powerful, and most of us have more than one skill. We usually keep at least one hidden from everyone but our enforcer team. This secrecy is a habit that's very hard to break. Even with the people we love.

"Very soon," I whisper against her lips like a vow. "I won't have a single secret that doesn't belong to you."

CHAPTER 4

"WHERE ARE YOU GOING?" MAI, her voice a sleepy whimper, rolls over and latches her arm around me, trying to stop me from leaving the bed. The sheets I just pulled up to her shoulder slip down to her bare hips.

It's 4:45 a.m. Or so the cool blue numbers of the bedside clock tell me.

A soft sigh leaves her lips as my mouth presses a light kiss underneath her jaw. "Just across the hall. Only for a little while."

For me, it'll be a little while, but for her, it'll be the rest of the night. Sleep is done for me. My body only requires about two hours' worth, and I've reached my max at nearly three. After our breakfast picnic in the park, we stumbled into the apartment for hours of skin-clawing sex that left us both exhausted. Now my body is re-energized and too restless to stay in bed anymore.

With two months of sleeping in the same bed, Mai already knows this. Doesn't mean she likes it, though. I kiss her again. "When you wake up later, we can have sex for breakfast."

She makes some noises of agreement and snuggles under the thin covers, apparently satisfied with my answer.

I shuffle my way down the hall and past things on the walls that have gradually expanded from simply her things to ours. A framed photo of me and my sister. Two pairs of Aztec warrior masks, one set in gold and the other in turquoise. A miniature shawl my Tia Ana knitted for me when I was a child. These things of mine blend seamlessly with Mai's travel photos, some small paintings she's gathered over the years, and other things she's shifted to make room for me.

Sometimes I think that I should probably get my own place. I'm spending way too much time here for someone who's not paying the mortgage or Netflix bill. Mai hasn't said anything about me being that one-night stand who just never left. In fact, since I came home with her from her first and only trip to the place in Mexico I call home, she's been making noises about me living here with her forever.

But that's just a little too much for a two-month relationship. Even if we are lesbians. Or queer. Or whatever.

Looking at the pieces of our lives woven together on the walls of her home, I realize I'm not going anywhere.

In her quiet office, I sit at the desk and open my laptop.

My inbox for Professor Xóchitl Bentley looks like I haven't checked it in days. Student pleas for extra time on papers. Administrators at the college telling me how to run my classes. Emoji-laden subject lines shouting about the hot single ladies in my area.

Even though I cut back to part-time hours at the university—mostly teaching online seminars and with only one face-to-face class during the week—my email load seems the same as before. Too damn much. After erasing most of the messages, I switch to my encrypted enforcer mailbox.

Only three messages. Good.

Sometimes email seems like such a primitive way for the enforcers to communicate when we're not officially on the job. But it's also nice that I don't have to immediately respond or look someone in the face (or mind) when I'd rather be doing something else.

Obviously, I have a love-hate relationship with my work email.

The first email is a group message from Farr, one of the enforcers on my team, to the rest of us. I click on it, and a video of a cat trying to run up a plastic playground slide starts playing to the music of 50 Cent's "In Da Club." The video ends pretty much the same way it starts, with the cat in the same place it started. I snort laugh and reply with a middle-finger emoji.

The subject line of the second email drains the smile from my face. *Redstone Hearing.*

It's from the office of the Chief Enforcer of the North American region: basically, my boss, Wren Tall Trees, the gravel-voiced woman who's in charge of all three commander-led enforcer teams in North America and the sub-commanders and their teams under us.

Reflexively, I glance toward the door and the room where Mai is sleeping peacefully before opening the message. A thorough reading of the email tells me things I don't want to know—or to be true.

> *Commander—The trial for Ethan Redstone will be in one month. Your presence as one of the arresting officers is required during these proceedings. Through a change in protocol, the family will be allowed to speak in the criminal's defense, and their words have the potential to affect the ultimate outcome. See details of time and place below.*

A muscle is ticking in my jaw, and my fingers curl into the edge of the computer until it creaks. After all the time and effort I put into finally catching the man who killed my sister, just the word of his family might "affect the ultimate outcome?"

That's bullshit.

A loud crash jerks me to my senses—a glass apple from the desk shattered against the wall. Flung by me. My hitching breath fills the room, and my chest feels like it's about to crack in two. I force myself to calm down.

This isn't the time to lose it.

Ethan Redstone has been in a holding cell at the North American enforcer headquarters for months now. For as long as Mai and I have been officially together.

That's not normal.

Enforcers don't keep prisoners. Holding cells are meant to keep a captive for a few days, weeks at the most. Not up to a month. Hearings, usually held within days or weeks of criminals being caught, are usually a formality. When we find a criminal, we know without a doubt that they are guilty. We don't strike until we are certain. Ethan Redstone is guilty, no matter how many members of his family they can scrape together to say how good he is at water polo and doesn't deserve to die.

He may not be guilty of all the charges—certainly not of being the Absolution Killer—but he did kill helpless Meta children. He tried to kill Mai. He killed my sister.

The memory of the day that I found Ixchel rises up, an agony. Her body broken, discarded on the side of the road like trash. Brown eyes frozen wide and empty. From her mother, I discovered she was missing, tracked her, but found her too late. My failing. My fault.

I can't fail her again. I won't.

My vision goes red, and the room around me wavers like I'm seeing it through a haze of intense heat. The blood rushes like liquid fire through my veins, and it's like I can feel every pathway my blood burns, every organ it feeds.

Ethan Redstone.

When I tracked him down with every intention of killing him, I didn't give a damn who his family was. When I ripped his father apart with my bare hands, I cared even less. Men like these don't get to wreak havoc on the world, my world, and get away with it.

The sound of burning plastic drags my mind back to the here and now. In my hand. The computer mouse is nothing but melted pieces of black plastic dripping down between my fingers and all over the desk.

Shit. I can't be a freeloader *and* the one who breaks her girlfriend's stuff.

The chair jerks across the floor with a squeal as I jump to my feet and start cleaning up the mess. The burnt mouse and broken paperweight. It doesn't take long for me to finish up and get back to checking my email.

Thank God the rest of it is boring. More of the usual.

Our weekly, in-person briefing is coming up in a few days. Then there's a request from a team out west for a standby backup in case they need help putting down a Meta who's been drinking human and Meta blood in Vegas.

A big part of my job as an enforcer is to stay ready. Sometimes watching and investigating, but mostly waiting in the wings like some invincible, fire-breathing dragon ready to burn away any signs of infection in the Meta communities. This waiting gives us a lot of free time to get into a little trouble on our own.

Speaking of trouble...

My thoughts drift again to the woman sleeping nearby. My lover. My heart. She needs to know about her cousin's idiotic hearing, and the sooner the better. But am I going to be the one to tell her?

Yes. I have to be. I won't treat her like glass. I won't lie to her.

A few minutes later, I slip into bed next to Mai and pull her body back against mine. Making soft, sleepy sounds, she reaches for me, her fingers slipping up my neck and into my hair. Her butt wriggles into the cradle of my hips, and she sighs. She smells like sleep and contentment. Neither of which will last long when I tell her what I need to.

I take a deep breath. Any possibility of the promised breakfast sex is about to evaporate like water on hot pavement.

But when we came together to make this thing work, we promised no secrets, no lies.

"Mai." With a firm grip, I still the provocative motion of her hips before it makes me lose my nerve. "There's something you need to know, and I don't think you'll like it."

CHAPTER 5

"Do you think it's true that Professor Bentley and Mai Redstone are fucking?" a male voice asks from nearby. "I hope so. That would be kinda hot."

The student papers I just gathered slip from my hands and scatter all over my desk.

What?

I know who it is. Michael, a student from my class just letting out, is halfway down the hallway and practically out of the building, but my senses are trained to pick up any mention of Mai's name now.

"Stop being disgusting. They're both like thirty or something," his friend, a girl I've never had in my class, responds with a sound of revulsion.

Michael snorts. "You don't think that way when you're stalking Professor Green on Instagram and writing fan fiction about him online."

"That's different. He's such a DILF, crazy sexy..."

The two students keep walking, and I allow their voices to fade away. A sweep of the minds around them yields not even the slightest curiosity about their conversation. Damn, they really have nothing better to talk about. With a shake of my head, I pick up the scattered essays and slip them into my bag. More work for my TA to deal with later.

Right now, it's lunchtime and I have a date.

It doesn't take me long to reach the little Lebanese restaurant near campus. It's close enough that the bright purple high heels I wear with my gray shift dress don't get the chance to start truly hurting my feet.

The smell of roasting meat greets me at the restaurant door. It smells nice enough, but what I wouldn't give for a platter of *chiles rellenos* right now.

Immediately I spot Mai sitting at a small table at the back of the small restaurant. Her back is to the wall, she has a half-finished glass of water in front of her, and at her feet is her school briefcase, probably full of student papers to start grading if I showed up any later.

She and I haven't talked much about her cousin's upcoming hearing other than to confirm we'll both be there. Mai is frightened and furious, but she's released all that for now so we can enjoy each other and the life we're building together. Still, the specter of the hearing hovers over us. It's only a matter of time before it pounces.

That time is not today, though.

"Hello, lovely."

Her answering smile lights up my whole world.

They're wondering about us. My thought slips seamlessly into Mai's mind as I lean down to kiss her mouth in greeting.

"As long as it's just speculation and they don't know anything for sure, it shouldn't matter."

It doesn't matter anyway, I want to tell her but don't. To me, this human job and identity are disposable. But she doesn't feel the same. It's her way to escape her family and so much more.

My lips seek hers again. My way of letting her know that our mini-discussion is over. Her teeth sink into my lips before pulling back. She's smiling.

Like a fool, I smile right back. "What are we trying today?"

Mai has made a game out of discovering things about each other and this new world we share. The goal is to take nothing for granted. So we're trying every restaurant near the university together and also trying everything on the menu. At times, it's been a little horrifying. Mai's palate thinks most food is different and interesting and to be savored. But everyone knows Mexican food is the best food.

"I'm not sure," she says. "I've been looking at the menu while you took your sweet time getting here"—Mai nudges my foot under the table to let me know that she's joking—"but I haven't decided yet."

"Why don't you pick something for us?" Like most of the places we've stumbled into so far, this doesn't seem like my kind of food. But with Mai, I'm open to trying anything. The drinks look far more interesting. After a quick glance at the menu, I already know what I'll get for us.

I think it gives Mai a thrill when I tell her what "we" want. There's a swing in her slender hips as she saunters up to the counter to order. As usual, she looks both elegant and sexy in her "professional" clothes. Although she seems to have no idea, the outfit of a black, high-collared dress with the red belt and matching heels have dominatrix all over it. No wonder she stars in half her students' masturbation fantasies.

As I reluctantly pull my gaze away from her backside, I catch a glimpse of someone vaguely familiar. Cropped yellow blouse, jeans. Hair in braids. Oh yeah. A student I ran into in the hallway near my office earlier. Once identified, my senses release the details of the girl and her nagging sense of familiarity. We're near the university; of course there's bound to be a student or ten at these little cheap restaurants nearby.

"Hey, you want to help me with these?" Mai calls to me a few minutes later from the counter. Our entire order looks ready and seems like far too much to carry on her own.

"Coming, darling." Like a good little wife in training, I rush to do her bidding.

"You're not fooling anyone with that act," she says when I meet her at the counter and pick up the overflowing tray. She gets our drinks and heads back to our table, hips swaying like a dinner bell.

"Are you sure? What if I let you—what do the kids call it—top tonight? Would that prove to you how completely devoted and sincere I am?"

She almost drops the paper cups full to the brim with our drinks. Jallab, according to the menu. Something fruity that smells like roses. "Stop playing with me." Mai goes to sit down, and I watch because it entrances me every time she does it. Slowly bending, she slides one full butt cheek on the chair, then slides all the way over with an intriguing motion of her hips. This woman makes sitting down into an art, or at least one of the chapters of the *Kama Sutra*.

I show her my sharp teeth. "If you think this is playing, wait until tonight."

Mai purses her lips and settles the tray more evenly between us, the drinks like exclamation marks on both sides of our plates of food. Her butt wriggles a bit more in the chair, and I've no doubt she's doing it to me on purpose.

"I thought you said you'd let me top tonight?" she asks with a smirk.

The piece of kibbeh I put in my mouth is unexpectedly nutty and delicious. It slides over my tongue like a deep-fried dream. "You do know if I have to *let* you top, we're already in trouble."

Her tongue pokes out at me, and I laugh. Mai tears off a piece of the bread and eats it slowly enough to make it a tease. Her fingers are slick from the oils in the bread. She puts those glistening fingers in her mouth, one by one, and licks them off, eyeing me the whole time. Of course, she grins when I nearly swallow my tongue watching her.

It's been an unexpected bit of paradise getting to know her and allowing her to see some real parts of me. Before meeting her, the thought of being with someone who challenges me and makes me want to shift and accommodate their presence in my life was about as appealing as childbirth. But now, if she cracked my chest open and examined me from brain to tiny toes, I'd tell her that she missed a spot just to get her to spend more time giving me her full attention.

Mandaia-Pili Redstone. My lover. My heart.

She's nothing like the woman who gave birth to her and named her. She's better.

They're both beautiful and powerful Metas with complete willingness to use the very limits of these powers to protect the people they love. But while Mandaia is a hammer, Mai is a slow-working poison. By the time you realize just how dangerous she is, it's far too late to do anything about it.

But my woman's poison is kindness and mercy, and I've only just started to realize how dangerous those things are to me, and how far beneath her spell I've fallen.

CHAPTER 6

"Just for the record, I don't want to be here." Although it's pure silk, the spaghetti-strap dress feels uncomfortable on my otherwise bare body. Stirred by the wind from the balmy evening, the hem flutters around my knees as light as a new lover's touch.

"You've already said that," Mai says, and presses the doorbell to her family home. "Eight times since we got in the car. Maybe even nine."

The half-dozen silver bangles along my arm chime with the sound of warning bells when I put my hand on the small of her back. "Just so you don't have any false expectations about tonight. I'm not here to make nice with them but I promise at least not to embarrass you." Then I remember the people who make up her family and what their expectations probably are. "At least not on purpose."

"Don't worry, I'm not deluded." Despite my churlishness, Mai leans in to me with a smile on her red-painted lips. She's wearing all black tonight, slim-fitting slacks, and a blouse that makes the red on her mouth especially distracting. "Thank you for coming with me tonight. I can't tell you how much this means to me."

I don't even know how I agreed to this. One second, we were in bed talking about her cousin's upcoming farce of a hearing, Mai's body shivering with sympathetic rage against mine, and the next, I was promising I'd go with her to her family's next dinner thing.

How was I supposed to know it was so soon? A week doesn't seem like enough time to prepare for something like this.

"You're not welcome, Mandaia-Pili Redstone."

A pinch of my side lets me know—again—how much she hates being reminded that she's named after her mother.

Despite the bright color on her lips, which is probably called something like "Don't Kiss Me Kate," I pull her closer and press my mouth to hers. The feel of the matte lip color is powder smooth, and I sigh with pleasure when her lips part and give me just the smallest bit of suction along with the distant flavor of the mint toothpaste Mai used before we left her condo.

Pussy-whipped. That's the only reason I'm dressed like I'm really here to meet the parents and make nice instead of ripping every single one of their throats out.

But Mai wants me to be good, so here we are.

The front door opens just as I lean in to kiss the perfect curve of her mouth one more time. Delicately sweet, the scent of a thousand flowering plants flows out from the house to meet us.

"Mai, you're on time for once." Instead of one of their many maids, it's her brother, Cayman, who answers the door. "And you brought company. Come on in."

My mind automatically retrieves the basic information I know about him.

Cayman Gregory Redstone. Second born of three children to his parents, Mandaia and Quinn Redstone. Thirty years old. Moderately powerful telekinetic and dissatisfied mama's boy. If Mandaia asked him to murder a hospital full of Meta babies, the only question he'd ask is, "Should I make them suffer?"

That last is only my opinion, of course.

He's wearing designer jeans and a dress shirt under a tweed jacket with elbow patches. Clothes for a semi-formal dinner, just as advertised. I half expected them to tell Mai it was semi-formal while everyone else showed up in pearls and tuxes. Just to make her look less-than.

Cayman's assessing look down my body is probably meant to get some sort of reaction out of me. The little bastard is no better than the rest of his family, so I don't waste a smile or anything else on him. He steps back to allow us across the threshold of their home, a house protected by human security systems as well as those designed by Metas, engineered to counter any human or Meta methods of trying to break in.

"Good evening, Cayman. Lovely to see you as always." Mai sidesteps her brother's attempt at kissing her cheek and loops an arm around my waist. "This is Xóchitl Bentley. I told you and Mother I would invite her to dinner with us."

Things are supposed to be better between Mai and her brother now. Months ago, when he found out that their cousin Ethan was a murdering, sadistic piece of trash who'd fooled nearly everyone else in the family into believing he was just a normal Redstone—whatever that is—Cayman was shocked.

From what Mai found out and later told me, he hated that he was manipulated by his cousin, and by his uncle, who also happened to be another murdering, sadistic piece of trash. It was my pleasure to take out the garbage. He said he was sorry, and Mai thought that meant their relationship was about to change for the better. But it's been a slow process.

Cayman tosses off a bow in my direction in acknowledgment of the introduction. "Of course, your colleague at the university. Isn't fraternizing against the rules over there?"

"Since when do you care about human rules, Cayman?"

"I don't, but I know you do. Something that never ceases to amaze me." He shuts the door with a muffled bang. "Especially now that your increased powers show you just how much better than them you are."

Mai rolls her eyes and pushes past him into the massive foyer, her arm still around my waist. A look over my shoulder confirms Cayman's eyes are glued to my ass. I wonder if he'd do the same thing if I was his brother's girlfriend instead of his sister's.

While the siblings exchange their version of pleasantries, I look around the house. Of course it's an impressive and huge thing with marble in all the right places, and a spiral staircase leading from the foyer and up to mysterious rooms above. Orchids in a rainbow of colors, delicate vines dripping with pale flowers, and blooms of every imaginable type perch in corners of the grand hall and from the ceilings.

The flowers are beautiful and smell like a piece of paradise, but when touched by Mandaia's power over all things in nature, they become pretty weapons. Vines that she can grow to the size of trees to kill and destroy. Soil she could force down someone's throat and choke them to death. The possibilities are endless and oh-so delightful.

This house is everything I expect of Mandaia Redstone, head of the powerful Redstone Family and North American Meta matriarch.

As an official resident of North America, I'd been technically welcomed to the annual Conclaves held here. These are big annual gatherings of the Families of the region where important unions, decisions, and even births are announced. Some couples even choose to get married at Conclaves. Then there's a gigantic party.

But my family isn't an important one to include in any of the main events, and after Ixchel was killed, I became more closed off, staying in Mexico with my aunts and the various cousins except when I was away on enforcer business. Or business of my own.

And now, here I am, in the house of the man who killed my sister, among people who would gut me where I stand if they knew who I was and what I'd done.

The things I do for love.

"Mai!" A shriek of happiness comes from the top of the marble stairs. "I wasn't sure you'd come!"

A woman, very nearly just a girl, runs down the staircase still speaking in exclamation marks. This has to be Mai's little sister, Abi. Twenty-three years old and just broken up with her Swiss boyfriend. Recently moved back home from Switzerland and spending time trying to get to know her sister whom she'd been separated from by years of boarding school and family drama.

Still happily babbling, she throws her arms around Mai just as I step out of the way to prevent myself from being the casualty of a too-enthusiastic hug.

"This is actually perfect," Abi says, laughing in her happiness. She has to look up at Mai who is even taller in what I call her dominatrix heels. "I was going to text you and ask about this new movie that's showing at the arts cinema. It's all weird and lesbian-y. I think you'll love it."

"Sounds perfect. Why don't we have tickets already?" Mai smiles through the hug, holding her sister just as tightly as Abi holds on to her. There's a desperation there that's beautiful to see.

"Because I was hoping I'd see you and invite you in person. Texts are great but seeing you is a thousand times better."

The girl looks so happy that it seems fake. But maybe it's because I don't expect any sort of authentic emotion from a Redstone other from anger or uncontrolled vice. Mai excepted, as always. The two women keep talking—well, Abi does, while Mai indulges her. A smile on her face, like she's looking at her daughter instead of her sister.

At first glance, the two women don't look anything alike. With her thick afro and agate skin, cuffed slacks, and high heels, Mai looks delectable. Both severe and sexy.

In her green West African-print jumpsuit and with her loose curls tumbling around her bronze and glowing face, Abi looks like the happiness Mai should've had as a child.

"Come meet Xóchitl," Mai says between one of her sister's enthusiastic bursts of words. She moves a hand behind her like she doesn't have to look to see where I am, and because I am always close enough for her to touch, I grasp her fingers in mine. "She's the woman I told you about."

"Oh! She's gorgeous!" She leaps away from her sister with a soft laugh. "Please excuse my bad manners, Xóchitl." Abi throws out both hands to clasp mine and pull me just the tiniest bit closer to herself and away from Cayman who's still watching us.

Is it my imagination? No. Her mind is as blank to me as most Metas, but her body language is clear. She's wary of her brother. Why, I wonder...?

"Thank you for the welcome, Abi. Your sister dragged me here by the ears, but I'll endeavor to be as polite as possible."

Her eyes widen the tiniest bit. "Honest, aren't you?"

"I try to be, unless lies are necessary."

She flicks a gaze to Mai and rolls her eyes. "Of course you'd bring home someone as impossible as you." My hand drops from hers. "Come on, let's go into the salon while they're getting dinner ready."

A peek at the massive clock perched among other antiques on the walls tells me it's exactly the time Mai was told dinner was to start. I bite back a sigh. Socializing before the food. Right. People do that.

Mai's fingers link with mine, and the three of us lead Cayman toward a set of doors off to the left. It's a salon, a bit more low-key than the foyer and its impression of extreme wealth and luxury forced on visitors. The long, L-shaped leather sofa is the shade of fine tobacco. A pair of forest-green velvet armchairs littered with yellow pillows and the Turkish rug spread over the hardwood floor give the room a welcoming impression of color. The tall windows show off views of the wide porch, the night-muted grassy hill, and the road leading down to the end of the gated courtyard. Flowers and vines rest in built-in nooks all over the place.

And, of course, Mandaia Redstone reigns over it all.

Her husband is in the room as well, but despite his impressive Meta powers, with his wife so close, he is easy to overlook. He's dressed more or less in the same way as Cayman and looks resigned to being here.

Mandaia sits on one of the large, high-backed velvet armchair like a queen on her throne. Her smooth skin and midnight-black shoulder-length curls betray not even a hint of her fifty-four years. A simple butter-gold dress shows off her slender but curvaceous figure and high, black heels complete the look. As we walk into the room with Abi chattering away, she smoothly stands.

"Mandaia-Pili."

Mai winces but attempts a smile. "Mother." With a grace that mirrors her mother's, she crosses the room to exchange a light press of cheeks while Abi watches them, smiling, her hands clasped in front of her. If not for Abi's reaction and the fact that I know Mai hasn't been together with the entire family like this in months, I could be fooled into thinking this is normal.

"I need a drink." Cayman heads to the bar where his father stands pouring whiskey into a nearly empty glass. He takes the bottle once his father is finished with it and makes himself an impressive drink over ice.

"I'm happy you made it, Mai," her mother says with a light squeeze of her hands.

"Well, I'm glad we could all finally get together like this." A minute shift happens on Mai's face, a hint of her slight unease with this new detente.

Damn. I want more for her. But she'll never get it from these people.

Mai clears her throat. "Mother, meet Xóchitl. She's the woman I'm seeing. I think it only makes sense for you two to meet."

What she doesn't say is that if I'd been human, she never would have brought me here. Politics in the Meta world can crush an unwary or oblivious human. Not to mention the games we play that always end up being for keeps.

"Madam." I nod my head in acknowledgment of Mandaia Redstone and her power. Nothing else. "Thank you for welcoming me into your home."

"Wait." For a moment, a tiny line links her eyebrows. "I know you."

"No, you don't."

All sounds stop in the room. No clinking of the ice in Cayman's glass. No breaths. Even Abi's mindless chatter stops.

Mandaia doesn't know me. She's seen me before, though. Dressed as an enforcer, masked, and pissed off while arresting her nephew for murder. Caught up in the adrenaline of the moment, I took my mask off then. But the face I showed to her and the rest of the people in that room wasn't my real one.

"You seem very sure," Mandaia finally says, her eyes more assessing the longer she looks at me.

My jaw clenches. I should've kept my mouth shut but even at the best of times, that's hard for me.

Mai clears her throat. "She's just very plain speaking, Mother. I'm sure you remember what that's like."

I slide her a narrow-eyed look.

There's no need to apologize for me, I send to her. *I said what I said. It may have been ill-advised but I damn sure won't take it back.*

Mai's lips press tight. *Xóchitl, please!*

Swirling gold eyes the same shade as Mai's try to dissect me. Not looking away from me, Mandaia says, "I'm sure she can speak for herself, daughter."

"That I can certainly do," I agree without blinking.

Really, I should keep a low profile, especially with the secrets I'm trying to hide, but this family makes me want to burn everything in sight to the ground.

"Um." Abi looks between me and her mother. Confusion and discomfort catch her lower lip between her teeth, but she seems determined to do something about settling the tension in the room. She heads toward the bar where her father and Cayman still stand. "Would you like a drink, Xóchitl? Mai?"

Mai looks like she wants to pinch a few pounds of flesh off my hide, but she still steps toward me, a hand held out to take mine. "That would be—"

"Sorry I'm late, everyone. Did I miss anything?" A woman stands in the doorway with a hand perched on her hip. Long hair, loose and dark, down to her hips. A figure-hugging maroon dress. Ballet flats. Her smile is perfectly bright and perfectly sharp, every inch a Redstone.

I brace myself to face yet another one.

38

CHAPTER 7

FROM THE WAY THE NEW woman is just standing there, it's obvious she thinks she's blazingly gorgeous. Her teeth flash with amusement, and her dark green eyes touch every one of us like she's imagining taking us each to her bedroom. Everyone except Mandaia Redstone.

"Caressa." Cayman is the one who greets her. "We were wondering if you were even going to show up." He raises his drink in her direction, and his smile is welcoming enough.

After greeting Mandaia with an oddly formal bow, the woman slips across the salon to pluck the drink from Cayman's hand. "Hopefully this is for me," she purrs. "After the day I've had fighting with the other Republicans in DC, I really need a drink." The sip she takes from the glass is dainty enough, but she doesn't blink at how strong it is. "They need a healthy dose of leadership up there, people who lead with power and strength instead of this ridiculous *compromise*."

She says the last like it's a dirty word.

Mai rolls her eyes and moves toward the woman. "It's good to see you, Caressa. I didn't realize you were coming to dinner with us tonight." She looks briefly at me, then offers an answer to the question I hadn't asked yet. "She's one of the family, a cousin."

Although I nod, I don't need Mai to tell me who this is. Months ago, I memorized the Redstone family tree, even the more obscure branches. Caressa Redstone MacTavish is a fifth cousin, related to Mai by only a hint of blood. Officially, she's an empath, level four at most. She's also an American senator. At forty years old, she's one of the youngest, and apparently one of the most influential behind the scenes. Already I can tell she's going to be annoying.

I manage something that resembles a smile in the cousin's direction. "The more the merrier."

"I'm afraid I invited myself." Caressa exchanges brief hugs with Mai. "I'd heard you were coming over and since we haven't seen each other since the Conclave last year, well…" She shrugs, smiling down at Mai in a way that should make my hackles rise but instead only makes me wonder why she's trying so hard.

Caressa gently disengages herself from Mai and makes it over to me, drink still in hand. "You must be the new woman Mai's been talking about non-stop." Her eyebrow arches, and there's definitely flirtation in her smile.

We exchange proper greetings, and I quickly move back at her attempt at the European double cheek kiss. Her perfume is strong. I don't want it on my clothes.

"It'll be interesting getting to know you." I take her hand and give it a single, firm shake.

"Since you're here and meeting the family, I'm guessing you're… one of us?" The question tilts up at the end, and I smile at its clumsiness. She holds onto my hand longer than necessary before letting it go.

"Something like that." I tuck my hands to safely behind my back.

From the peanut gallery, Cayman makes an impatient sound. "Of course she's one of us. Even my sister isn't stupid enough to bring a human here." Then he looks up from pouring himself another drink, his gaze narrowing at Mai. "You're not, are you?"

A flash of annoyance burns bright inside Mai, but she turns her back on her brother without bothering to reply. Her fingers ghost over my arm, a grounding touch for both of us. "He's always been a little slow," she says to me.

Cayman snarls.

Abi appears at my side with a pair of drinks. The one she hands me is Bailey's on ice. "I hear you like it sweet and creamy," she says with a cheeky grin before offering Mai a glass of white wine.

Mai pokes her sister in the arm and hides a smile with the rim of her wine glass. "Ignore Abi," she says to me. "She's just being a brat."

How she can smile in this house of rabid dogs is beyond me, but that curve of her mouth does something to me. My fingers twitch from the desire to pull her close and, despite the off-putting company, taste the smile on her vermillion lips. Instead, I put the glass of Bailey's to my mouth. The creamy flavor of it is almost as intoxicating as Mai's.

"You *are* one of us, but I haven't seen you at a Conclave before." Mandaia Redstone has not moved from her improvised throne, and she hasn't taken her eyes from me during the entire time we've all been having our strange little conversations. "I'd remember if you had been."

Whatever it is I've popped loose in her memory, she's not letting it lie. But I won't give her the satisfaction of any type of closure, especially since what she's trying to recall is probably a time when she shouldn't have noticed me.

"Pardon me, everyone." A curvy and low-voiced woman wearing some sort of uniform—black pants and a white blouse—appears in the doorway. Once we all look her way, she bows. "Dinner is ready to be served."

Saved by the dinner bell.

After a quick glance at his wife, Quinn Redstone gestures to the open doors of the salon. "Shall we adjourn to the dining room?"

I look away from Mandaia and her hawk's eyes.

We all leave the room, following the uniformed woman into a small dining room a few doors away. The rectangular eight-seat dining table is set for seven, and the lights are brightly lit. Once Mandaia settles at the head of the table and her husband to her right, the rest of us flow silently into whatever chairs are left, leaving the opposite end of the table empty. Somehow, Caressa ends up sitting directly across from me.

Once we're seated, more servants appear with food. They leave behind a basket of warm bread in the middle of the table along with delicate bowls full of what looks like pumpkin soup. Soup and bread. Before we left her apartment, Mai warned me to expect at least a five-course meal.

Five. Jesus…

Food doesn't usually make me sad, but tonight is an exception. Only four more courses to go. The crisp white napkin I drape across my lap feels like a shackle trapping me in the chair.

Under the cover of the table, Mai squeezes my thigh. Her thoughts of comfort drift over me.

Why couldn't we have stayed in bed all day reading to each other and making love like I planned? Oh, because I promised her I'd be part of this dumpster fire instead.

"So do you like teaching at the university, Xóchitl?" Quinn Redstone picks up a piece of bread and dips it into his soup. His flat smile begs me to grab this conversational ball and run with it.

The man obviously doesn't want to be here any more than I do.

"I'm only there part time, but I do enjoy it, yes." Following his lead, I take one of the hot pieces of nut bread, but instead of dunking it into the soup, I tear it into little pieces. Crumbs fall on the table in front of me. "The students are interesting and it's fun watching most of them stumble all over themselves to impress Mai."

"Is that right?" Cayman doesn't look interested in the question though, like he can't imagine anyone fascinated enough by his sister to try and impress her. Obviously, he lacks imagination.

"Yes. She brings out those sorts of feelings in a lot of people." I show him some teeth, drop the pile of shredded bread into the soup, and slowly begin to eat it. "Me included."

Mai bites the corner of her pouty mouth to hide her bashful smile.

"You guys are so cute! I could just eat you up." Caressa meets my eyes as she takes a sip of her whiskey. Then winks at Mai.

Yes, trying way too hard.

"I respect that Mai inspires such affection in her students, but that's the age when educators and students are so close in age and experience that it becomes dangerous." Quinn continues on like the byplay between me and his son didn't happen. Or as if Caressa hasn't spoken. "Every other day it seems like we're hearing about some terrible student/teacher goings-on."

"It does happen, true enough," I reply. "Practically every day rumors swirl around campus about some professor and a student, but usually nothing comes of it. The students are usually over eighteen, and the people who should punish these professors are so used to it happening that they overlook it."

That sounds like something an invested educator would say, right?

"That's unfortunate," Mai's father says. Obviously, he couldn't care less.

The conversation tapers off after that, the silence broken only by the sounds of utensils against cutlery, wine being poured. Then the servants come again in another wave, taking away the empty soup bowls and replacing them with beet salads and more bread.

"Mai…" Mandaia's fork sinks into the beets, and the deep red juice squirts everywhere, smearing red all over the white plate. "Did you know that Ethan's hearing is coming up?"

My hand tightens around my fork, but I keep eating as if I don't feel Mai tense beside me. Her mind was calm and coasting along on good feelings and positive thoughts just seconds ago. Now it's buzzing with some unpleasant emotion. She's trying to hide it from me but doesn't quite pull it off.

My fork pierces through a mound of sliced beets. The tines are bloody red.

"Yes." Under the table and out of sight, Mai's hand comes to rest on my thigh. "But I don't see how it concerns me."

"Your testimony is what put him in front of the hearing in the first place," Cayman says after exchanging a look with his mother. "Remember?"

"That's not something I'll ever forget," Mai says dryly. "*You* should remember that Ethan was trying to kill me when enforcers caught him in the act. I didn't have to say anything for them to take him away."

"Maybe that was all a misunderstanding." Caressa tilts her head, looking at Mai. "You know how excitable Ethan can get."

"*Misunderstanding?*" Mai echoes with a twist of her lips. "I don't think so."

"There is some doubt in the family that he killed Stephen. Ethan was a lot of things, but I do know for a fact that he loved his father." Mandaia speaks quietly between precise bites of her food. "Which means there is also doubt he is the Absolution Killer." She pauses, her lips tightening briefly. "That's why I'm going to testify in his defense, and I think you should, too."

Is this woman serious?

The knife and fork clatter from Mai's hands even before her mother finished speaking. Abi's mouth drops open. She opens and closes it a few times, but nothing comes out. Mai slips her hands into her lap and pins first her brother then her mother with an unforgiving gaze. I grip her trembling fingers. They are as cold as her mother's heart.

"Mom, think about what you're saying!" Abi finally gasps out. "You know what Ethan did. It's not some made-up story you can just ignore. People are dead. *Children* are dead." Her fingers dig into the expensive wood of the table, and the sound is nails-on-chalkboard loud. "He tried to kill Mai!"

Mandaia makes a dismissive motion that's meant to silence her younger daughter. It works all too well. Not so much on the older one, though.

"Is that why you invited me here tonight? To ask me to testify in Ethan's defense?" Mai's voice rings out in cold judgment. Her back is an iron rod. But I know her mother had just cracked her open and spilled out her insides for anyone to see.

"It wasn't the reason at first," Mandaia says, her face absolutely calm with no awareness of the damage she's doing to her child. Or maybe she just doesn't care. "But when we received the news about the hearing finally being scheduled after such a long delay, this seemed like the perfect time to have the conversation."

Quinn Redstone is looking at his wife like he doesn't recognize her. "You told me you weren't going to the hearing, Mandaia." His voice is a soft reprimand. "Much less try to convince Mai to go. You know what she went through with your brother and then with Ethan."

Caressa seems stunned but regards Mandaia with approval. Only Cayman looks completely unsurprised by this fucked-up turn in the dinner conversation. Watching the way he interacts with his mother, he seems to lean into every shift of Mandaia's breeze, supporting any agenda of hers, no matter how stupid. Or dangerous.

I abruptly put my fork and knife beside the plate and drop my napkin beside them. Under the table, I grab Mai's hand again and prepare to stand up. This has gone on long enough.

"You don't have to stay here and listen to any of this," I tell her, not bothering to keep my voice low.

Mai's fro quivers as she shakes her head. "It's okay. I need to hear this. I need to hear exactly how my mother plans to convince me to testify for someone who terrorized me and would have killed me if the enforcers hadn't come to stop him." Her chin juts out and a hint of a darker color appears along her jawline, then a rippling of skin as she unconsciously begins to transform.

Pain slices into my hand gripping hers. Streams of warm heat drip down my fingers. A quick glance under the table confirms what I'm feeling: blood, dark and red, floods between our joined hands and onto my dress.

Beyond her control, Mai's body is reacting to her stress and shock, becoming a weapon, becoming armor.

"It's okay, baby." I pour the calming whisper directly into her ear and slowly release her hand. "Try not to let them get to you."

The sharp gray spines that erupted from her hand slip out of my skin. Sluggishly, my flesh begins to knit back together. My fingers flex on my thigh, and the pain recedes like it never happened.

My silk dress is ruined. I know that much without looking too closely.

If I thought anything would come of it, I'd send the attempt at dry cleaning directly to Mandaia Redstone.

Just then, one of the silver bracelets on my arm vibrates, abruptly dragging my attention away from the drama happening at the dinner table. With a light tap of my bloodied finger, a long and narrow screen appears along the bracelet's edge. It's work. The "standby" about the Vegas blood drinker has become a "come get his ass." I've never been so happy for a rampaging, murderous Meta in my life.

But I want Mai to come with me.

After sending a quick reply, I tip my lips close to Mai's ear again. "I've got to go," I say softly. "You should come with too."

"I can't. Not yet." The pain is so raw in Mai's voice that I want to burn this whole house down and bury the entire family under the ashes.

Not that Mai will let me. This damn sense of duty she has...

I curse softly as my bracelet chimes again. "You don't owe them anything."

"But I owe this to myself." Her chilled fingers brush along my bare arm. "Go and take the car. They need you. I'll see you back home soon if they don't keep you."

"Fine." I get to my feet. "But you keep the car. I already have a ride." *We'll talk soon*, I tell her silently. "Thanks for the...interesting experience," I say to the table at large, stepping away. "But now I'm needed elsewhere."

"Right now?" Disappointment tugs down the corners of Abi's mouth. "But Mai needs..." She looks at her sister with obvious concern, which makes me almost like her.

"I know." But I have work to do.

Caressa looks from Mai to me, her forehead wrinkled in sympathy and some other emotion I can't name.

After a light kiss on Mai's frozen lips, I head for the front door, hating with every step that I'm leaving her behind to deal with this den of jackals on her own.

Behind me, a voice rises up. Cayman sounding disgruntled and petulant. "Where is she going in such a hurry?"

"It's work," Mai says coolly, and my heart squeezes at how broken she sounds.

"For real? Is there a grading emergency or something?"

"Stop being such a dick, Cayman." Abi's annoyed voice drifts after me. "I don't know what's gotten into you lately but it's not cute." Her throat clicks as she swallows. "Mom…"

I tune out the rest. It's pain by proxy, and I can barely deal with it. Not with leaving Mai there and knowing it's the type of pain she'll always run toward just because it's being inflicted by her family.

The front door of the mansion slams shut behind me, and I take in a lungful of breath, preparing to slip away. But a flash of awareness freezes me where I stand. There's someone very nearby who I didn't notice before. A Meta. They feel familiar, like they've been hovering at the edge of my attention for hours now. Maybe days.

As casually as I can, I turn and peer into the darkness but barely catch a brief outline of a figure before whoever it is darts away, running soundlessly over the grass and disappearing around the side of the house. My legs twitch, ready to give chase. But I can't. Not right now.

Spine rigid with tension, I look back toward the front door I just walked through.

Someone was just lurking on the grounds of the Redstone mansion. And there's no doubt in my mind that they followed Mai and me here.

CHAPTER 8

"I FEEL HOT AS FUCK, and not in a good way," Caleb mutters, adjusting his smooth black mask one more time, although I'm sure he doesn't really need to.

Through my own mask, he's a dark and effective-looking shape on the hotel roof near me. The lab-created material on all of our faces is completely breathable and designed for our comfort. Caleb is just fidgeting. As the best of us at mentally crafted illusions, he could just call up a blank image in front of his face for anyone who looks at him. But he wears a mask because we all wear masks.

The rest of the team quietly snickers at his discomfort, me included. Caleb is right, though. Right now, at a few minutes past 9 p.m., Las Vegas feels about as hot as the day. The city's blazing heat calls to the fire under my skin like comfort, and I know that Farr, the more powerful pyrotechnic on our four-person team, is in her element, too. Sitting in a corner on the hotel roof, she scans online traffic on a small handheld device for any signs of our perp.

"Still nothing," she says without looking up.

"Good news for us." Caleb grunts after giving his mask one last adjustment. Although Farr can scrub any digital information we don't want leaked, the less we have to manage, the better.

My team has been called in to help the West Coast-based enforcers catch Winston Gales, a particularly powerful Meta who'd let himself loose on the thrill-seekers of Sin City.

Like most Metas, Gales is pretty enough to get away with anything where most humans are concerned. He's been blessed with a sensual mouth, piercing eyes, and a body that's still muscled and at the peak of masculine perfection at the age of sixty-three. Enviable if he were human; just average as a Meta. But until very recently, he hadn't been trying his tricks on any Metas. It's just dumb luck on his part that he lured in a young Meta who could easily pass for a human.

He probably drank her blood expecting…whatever human blood tastes like and was in for a shock when the girl's very different flavor flooded over his tongue. He tried to hide the body but didn't have much luck with that, either.

"He says he's killing them because he loves them," Pascale, my second in command and our main teleporter, says as he scans the street.

If he ever wanted to, he could be a sub-commander in charge of his own team, but for some reason, he prefers to stick around here with me and the rest.

I roll my eyes at Pascale's words even though he can't see it under the full-face mask. "Sounds like one of my ex-girlfriends," I tell him from my crouched position on the very edge of the roof.

Settled in on top of a thirty-story hotel that blazes from top to bottom with pulsing lights, my team and I carefully watch the wide strip, searching for signs of the idiot we're here to catch. Well, we actually know where he is; we're just waiting on the main team in charge of the op to tag us in if things go south. From the urgent message we received that dragged us all out here, there's no other direction for this thing to go.

I hate being backup. There are at least ten more interesting things I could be doing right now, the most important of which is to be there for Mai. But I have to be here.

"Speaking of exes," Pascale says with his eyes still on the street below. Unlike the rest of us, he doesn't need binoculars to see what's going on down there. "Someone's been poking around and asking questions about you."

"I'm not surprised." From the other side of the roof, Caleb double checks his pockets to make sure the tranqs he put there earlier are still there and ready to go. He's always full of nervous tics while we're waiting on things to start, but once the action gets going, he's as steady as Gibraltar. "How many times has Xóchitl pissed off someone enough for them to want to stalk and kill her?"

I ignore him and the obvious amusement in his voice. "Who's been doing the looking?"

"Don't know." Pascale shrugs. "They didn't get very far but if someone already has an eye on you for whatever reason, you're not doing a good job of blending in."

"I don't think blending in is my problem." My mind flashes back to the uncomfortable dinner with Mai's family. Was one of them suspicious enough not to dismiss me as just a garden-variety asshole fucking their once-golden child? Thanks to my runaway mouth, Mandaia is definitely curious enough to poke around in my life. But she wouldn't have started before tonight.

"Just be careful," Pascale says. "They didn't get anything electronic or otherwise from us, but assume they're still looking."

"Thanks for the heads-up."

"No worries."

I frown down at the street, keeping an eye out for our perp, with my mind only ninety percent on the task at hand.

So, someone's been investigating me. In all the years I've been crossing boundaries whenever I wanted and skirting the legal edges of my job to get that very job done, this is the first time anything has come to my front door. Probably another consequence of being with Mai. As much as her family treats her like garbage, I strongly suspect they'd rip anybody apart who tried to do the same.

In-house terror only.

Still, I'm not absolutely certain it's the Redstones.

"Who's the girl he killed?" Farr asks, although she could easily find the information online. She's the other one on my team that is most like me in terms of strengths. She manages fire, too, but she can generate the explosiveness of a large bomb, while all I can do is just burn a person from the inside out—plus a few other low-energy tricks. Raised on technology and the internet, she can track anyone with any sort of digital footprint and was able to find Gales with little trouble when the other enforcer team asked for help. When they said "stand-by" to our team, they really should have told us to come in and do all the work.

Not that I can blame them. It's just that my team is more powerful than any available to run backup right now.

"A college student from an LA suburb. She was here with some human friends and seemed the tastiest of the bunch, so..." I hitch up a shoulder to indicate the murder, feeding, and subsequent regret.

Caleb looks up. "From a connected family?"

"Not that we can tell," Pascale chimes in. "Just one of us with barely there powers living on campus away from her family. She wanted her freedom."

That's not a desire I know about. My family has always been small: me, my sister, our parents, my aunts, plus the half a dozen cousins who floated in and out of the house in Mexico on their way somewhere else. Freedom from the people who love me isn't something I ever wanted. When my parents died in a car wreck along with one of my aunts, I held on to my sister more tightly than ever. Not that it did me any good.

"He's heading this way." Pascale suddenly points down to the street.

The rest of us move over to get a good look with our binoculars.

"The other team has eyes, too, but they're waiting to corner him in a less crowded place." Farr rolls to her feet and tucks away her handheld electronic scanner.

Below us, the strip is packed with tourists, business people, marriage mistakes waiting to happen. Gales is in the thick of things, strolling among the glitter and desperation like he doesn't have a care in the world. Certainly not like he's got a human bleeding out in a hotel room nearby or a dead Meta teenager on his conscience. But his deliberately nonchalant attitude says something else: It says he knows he fucked up taking the college girl. He knows he's on the enforcers' radar and it's only a matter of time before we reach him. He doesn't look like a man without a plan.

Among the crush of humans, a flash of dark against dark down below reveals the presence of someone from the other enforcer team. They're quiet and effective, just as we're all supposed to be, but that doesn't mean a thing with this guy. Gales's power is low grade but effective. Light telekinesis paired with self-healing. If he hadn't been tested as a child and found mentally unable to handle work as an enforcer, he could've been one of us.

Pascale lets loose a curse as the member of the other team falls back from following Gales. "They're not going to go for him."

Gales's hotel is nearby, and there are enforcers everywhere; he has to know that. The other team hasn't exactly been subtle about their presence. It doesn't feel like he's trying to avoid their obvious trap, either. What's his game?

"What the hell is he up to?" Caleb peers down with his enhanced goggles.

"That's not for us to think about," I mutter, but that's not true. Our place is to find a solution to the Gales problem if the other team doesn't, and so far they've been incompetent as hell in catching this low-powered killer. Obviously, he knows we're onto him. And he's up to something.

His suit is designer. His tie a pretty green against the crisp white of his shirt. He's dressed for someplace nice. He's not in a rush. He's... My eyes flicker down the strip ahead of him, on both sides of the street. Hotel. Bar. Casino. Concert hall. Another hotel—

Fuck me.

"Don't let him get any farther," I snap over the open communication with the other team. "A couple of blocks down on the left. There's a Meta family here from out of town. They're at Club Synergy." To be sure, I mentally scroll through the list of scheduled movements of the major Meta Families in the area. The Soyinkas. In a show of bad judgment, they have some sort of reunion here. Mandaia Redstone could teach them a thing or two about subtlety and keeping their family safe. They may have more powers than humans, but their bodies are still breakable. "Take him out now!"

"Hell," Farr growls through clenched teeth. "They won't do it."

None of the four members of the other team look close enough or ready enough to do what needs to be done. All night, their communications have been crackling with questions instead of orders, their new sub-commander too indecisive to bring down the hammer when necessary. Not that Farr should've been checking in on them, but it pays to be informed.

"Pascale, teleport down there with Caleb and shut this down." The two men are moving before I finish talking. "Caleb, make sure the humans don't notice me. Farr, scramble any cameras filming the action."

Already, I'm running to the edge of the building, the wind rushing against my face. A leap. My fingers catch on the edge, and I throw myself down the side of the building, surfing down the glass toward the street. Caleb's controlled burst of influence blankets the humans nearby just in case one of them looks up to see a figure in black sliding down a glass building.

Everything is perfectly normal. Caleb's words flow over the humans in a calming wave. Not a single person looks up.

Moments later, my feet hit the pavement and I slip into the dark, close to Gales. Quickly, I take off the dark mask covering my face, leaving only the facial-distortion disguise. If anyone looks, all they'll see is a woman wearing some sort of uniform with short hair, a forgettable face, and an attitude of everyday hurry.

Up ahead, Pascale is a few steps behind Gales. Caleb has knockout needles ready. Gales walks with a confident swing to his arms, looking rich and happy, normal enough for Vegas, but it's an attitude that attracts. *Look at me. I just won big.* And the humans are watching. Some with envy. Others with the clear intention of robbing him as soon as he steps into a dark corner.

He's good.

But not good enough.

Just a few feet away and I give Caleb the nod. The needles come out. One goes into Gales's thigh. He staggers and cries out, eyes darting around him, all the while turning to get away from the unexpected bite of the needle. Instantly, he sees Caleb.

To the humans, we blend in, but Gales knows what an enforcer looks like. Panic twists his face. But it doesn't stay long. Gales's power sends a woman's heavy-looking handbag flying into Caleb's throat, buckle first. Caleb dodges it, then slips to Gales's other side and stabs another needle into his back. He stumbles again, and Pascale is there to catch him.

People trip. It's a mass of confusion. But this is also Vegas; spontaneous theater happens on the streets all the time. People doing crazy things to draw attention and to pick each other's pockets. Easily ignorable. The other team should've known that and gotten to this idiot sooner. We can't afford to let him get to the club with whatever plans he's got as a backup.

"There. Into that alley!" But they don't get the chance to do much with Gales before he recovers again. *Right. Self-healing.* He sends a metal newspaper box flying. I dodge it, but a human man and his lady friend aren't so lucky. It smashes into them with a crunch. Bones breaking. Blood flying everywhere.

"End this shit now." A punch to the kidneys and Gales gasps loud. Instantly, Farr is there to clamp fire hot hands on him while Pascale stands near, ready to rip his body into pieces with his enhanced strength.

"Oh my gawd!" Farr shouts out with an exaggerated (and really bad) Southern accent. "Please excuse my husband. That raw seafood buffet really did him in!" And she drags him with Pascale's help, growling and spitting, into the alley. A pair of humans are already there, and the smell of sex rising from the cramped space tells me all I never want to know about what's happening between them.

Caleb shoves another needle into Gales on his way to rushing into the alley to roust the lovebirds on their way. They stumble out, one of the men still fumbling to drag up his jeans. Pascale throws Gales at Farr to go be the lookout, and Caleb takes his place.

Seconds later, the perp shivers to awareness, twists, and growls between Caleb and Farr. Caleb slams another needle into his neck. But he doesn't go down easily. Only a few seconds pass before he's fully aware again.

Dammit. With every knockout injection, his recovery time gets faster and faster.

"The human police are nearby," Pascale growls, keeping an eye out from the mouth of the alley. "We need to wrap this up quick."

But suddenly, a gray mist rises around Gales. Whatever is in it, instantly hits the back of my throat. A chemical burning.

"Poison!"

Like we've practiced a thousand times, we slip our masks on. The material used to hide our faces protects us from any poisons in the air as well. But I stumble anyway, knees hitting the concrete with a hard jolt I feel in my teeth.

This is Gales's plan against the family nearby. Since he already murdered the young girl and is basically a dead man walking, he wants to kill himself and take as many Meta with him as possible. Including the enforcers sent to catch him.

My vision clouds. My legs weaken.

No, no, *no*! Not the time. Not when I finally have the kind of life I've dreamed of for years.

Cursing Gales, I fumble for the cuffs behind my back and manage to get them around his wrists before he can move.

A tap on the controls at my wrist floods my body with a counter-poison inoculation. It hits me like ice, the feeling of frozen air overwhelming my lungs and blood. I shudder as my stomach lurches from the medicine. Gasping, I double over, bracing my gloved palms against the filthy ground. Footsteps race into the alley, and I stagger to my feet, ready to fight or bullshit my way through an explanation of what we're doing here.

But it's the other team, the original one that was supposed to stop this idiot in the first place. The four of them rush in like ants, swift and silent.

"Incoming," Farr growls from behind her mask. She shoves Gales down into the ground, face first, boot landing on his shoulders. He garbles as his nose and mouth land in a pothole full of stagnant water. But the sound of his breathing is weak. The poison he prepared is working almost too well.

If the primary team doesn't save him, self-healing power or not, he'll be dead in seconds.

Not our problem.

Farr steps back as the primary team rushes to surround our prisoner. Her spine is ramrod straight, and she looks invincible in her black clothes and behind her mask.

"We can take it from here," their leader barks.

No shit. With a flick of my wrist, I signal for my team to leave Gales's side and come to me. But the gas did a number on all of us, and it feels like a Mack truck is sitting on my chest. A vicious headache rings in my skull, and my body aches for water, dry enough to absorb an entire planet of fresh water. We're slow to regroup, but as soon as we're close enough to each other, Pascale opens a portal for us to flood through.

Seconds later, I reappear with my team in the room where we started the operation. A locked door. A table and four chairs. An open laptop attached to a projector showing the layout of Gales's hotel room. Farr collapses into one of the chairs, her head clutched in her hands. Caleb lurches away from the portal and slams into the wall before sliding down it to land on his ass. Pascale's nose is bleeding.

I manage to make it to the table before sagging back against it, the edge digging into my spine. Not remotely comfortable at all. Giving up on the painful lean, I drop down on the table's surface, flat on my back and staring up at the white ceiling. The bright lights feel like knives hacking at my eyeballs.

I squeeze my eyes shut.

"Shit. I thought this was supposed to be easy..." Pascale pants roughly, leaning against the wall, visibly shaking. He pulls off his masks, exposing his shaved head, goatee, and the sharp brown of his eyes.

"That's when you should've realized this whole operation was going to be shit," Farr mutters, her voice muffled by her hands still covering her face.

Caleb, with his head leaned back against the wall and his eyes closed, doesn't say a word. But his entire body looks like pain.

They're all ready to go home. Hell, I can't think of anyplace I'd rather be but Mai's rich-girl apartment, cuddled on the couch and dissecting what happened tonight at dinner. But we have a job to do. I pull in a deep breath and push it back out.

One by one, the rest of us yank off both sets of masks. Faces emerge, damp and overheated from the job, even Farr. Her close-cut natural hair glistens with sweat at the edges, and her full lips are tight with tension.

With an exhausted movement of his fingers, Caleb settles his thick red hair around his shoulders. A gray eye pops open to look at me.

"We need to find out where Gales got that poison from." I strip off my gloves, already dreading the time it's going to take. "It's not standard issue, and it's just too powerful to leave out there in the world."

A chorus of groans greets my announcement, but none of them disagree with me.

It's going to be a long night.

CHAPTER 9

I DON'T GET BACK TO Atlanta until nearly four in the morning.

With my body still cool from the shower I took at headquarters, I tiredly shed my clothes and slip into bed next to Mai. Her skin is warm and smells like the home she has become to me. When I settle under the covers facing her, her eyes stare back into mine.

"Was everything okay out there?" With a sleep-warm finger, Mai traces the damp edge of my hairline, then the whirl of my ear. "I was starting to worry."

"No reason for you to worry, Mai darling." I capture her wandering fingers and press them to my lips. "If anything, I was the one worried about leaving you in that house by yourself."

I feel her entire body flinch. "I wasn't alone," Mai says, defensive. "Abi was there."

That spoiled little flower? She can barely take care of herself with those people. If they ever decide to turn on her, too, she'd only whimper while they cheerfully destroyed her.

But I keep those words to myself.

"How long did you stay?" I ask instead.

"Not long. I left just a little while after you did. They...they really want me to testify for Ethan." The frown between her eyes looks painful. "It doesn't make any sense. They were so different before." She sounds so wounded and lost. My sweet love.

I kiss her fingers one by one as she watches me. "Do you want me to see what's going on?"

"It wouldn't make a difference." She shrugs, and it hurts me to see it, that small motion of resignation. "I don't know what could be wrong other than the—" A vicious shake of her head. "Anyway, I think Mother just changed her mind. Nothing and no one makes her do anything she doesn't want to."

I'm not so sure about that. No one is above influence. No matter how powerful a person seems, there's always someone out there with more leverage, more power, or less to lose.

"Shh. Don't think about it anymore tonight. Just rest." In the small amount of space between us, our fingers link together. "We'll deal with it tomorrow."

"Or never."

"Or never," I echo her words although I know avoidance isn't an option. Not where the Redstones are concerned. All this is about to come to a head. And very soon.

CHAPTER 10

"For what he's done, Ethan Redstone should die." The statement leaves my mouth as objectively as I can make it, but the hatred vibrates through my body. I'm sure everyone in the room can feel it.

"Thank you, Commander." The justiciar, a former enforcer himself, nods once from his place high on top of the bone-white dais, a symbol of enforcer justice, cold and merciless.

Mai sits with her family on one side of the justice box, an imposing and off-putting marble white square where her cousin sits trapped in a stasis field to prevent him from teleporting, his mouth held shut by someone's power while his eyes burn pure malice at everyone around him. I stand on the other side of the box with the rest of the enforcers who were there when Ethan was caught. They stand in an unbroken line next to me, legs braced apart, their faces covered, and utterly silent.

None of us should be here.

The job is done, and Redstone was caught about to murder his own cousin. He should be long dead by now. But after months of delays, here we are: the enforcers who were officially on the case and me, the one who chased and caught him. My leather gloves creak softly from the strain as I clench my fists.

At the sound, Mai darts a look across the room at me. Our eyes meet. Her distressed thoughts flow into mine. A gently cleared throat pulls Mai's attention back to the justiciar. Her mother reminding her of her manners and the reason she is here.

The Families have no control over what enforcers do. Justice is supposed to be above politics and power plays. But apparently, I can be naïve as Mai. I should have known that a family as powerful as the Redstones would have a say in what happens to one of their golden boys, even if his sheen has been tarnished.

Dozens of abusers and murderers have died for me to get to Ethan Redstone. Now, he's right in front of me, but I can't touch him. The courtroom is small, and there aren't many of us here, just enough for Ethan Redstone to seem so close yet so very far. I want to tear him apart.

The justiciar taps his gavel. "In light of the unusual circumstances with the accused's family, is there anything else the enforcers would like to add?"

Across the room and too far away for me to touch, Mai tenses up. Her family looks confident—Mandaia and Cayman, Caressa, plus the two others who've come to testify for Ethan Redstone. Abi sits next to Mai, holding her sister's hand.

What the hell else could there be for me to say? Then I get over myself and push away the anger clouding my thinking. The justiciar wouldn't ask unless there was something else at work that wouldn't make normal rules apply.

My boots are silent against the white marble floor when I step forward again.

"The on-scene enforcers caught Ethan Redstone in the act of trying to kill Mai Redstone. Ethan Redstone used instruments of torture on his cousin with deadly force. If we had not arrived in that key moment, the heir to Redstone would have likely been killed."

Obviously, that was laying it on a bit thick. Mandaia Redstone has two other children, one of them a woman. Given the relationship between Mai and her mother, the matriarch may very well use any legal means necessary to bypass the child she named after herself as heir. But few outside the family know that. Meaning nobody except for me.

"Thank you, Commander." The justiciar taps his gavel and dismisses me, allowing me to slip back into formation with the other enforcers. "Will anyone here speak on the criminal's behalf?" The justiciar sweeps an inquiring gaze around the room.

A pause.

"I will, Justiciar." Mandaia Redstone stands up for her nephew and simultaneously crushes everyone else under her heel.

The significance of what she's doing isn't lost on anyone. Mai's face doesn't change, but I can feel her sadness and the sickening kick of betrayal in her belly. It almost breaks me, but I force myself to stand still. Silent and impassive.

Mai needs someone with her to understand what she's going through. She's not like me.

"You don't have to stay here for this, Mai." Abi puts an arm around her sister, her own face naked with disappointment and surprise. Maybe she didn't really believe Mandaia would speak up for her nephew—and against her own daughter—until right now.

But Mai stays right where she is. Not responding to Abi, or at least not in words. She does stay under the comfort of her sister's arm and listens while her mother and then her brother defend Ethan Redstone and his actions.

Behind my back, my linked hands tighten into trembling fists. Heat rolls under my uniform, and the room feels like I'm watching it through a haze of fire.

I could kill them.

Very easily slip into that wide-open mansion of theirs and steal their lives the way Ethan Redstone stole my sister's. It wouldn't bring Ixchel back. It wouldn't take my woman's pain away. But it would make me feel better.

I feel the other enforcers in line with me begin to move restlessly. A whisper of cloth. Eyes shifting the bare amount to look at me. *Shit. I'm disturbing them.* Power hums under my skin, beginning to flow out into the room. It burns through me, sparking along my nerve endings and howling for release.

Normally, I have more control than this.

No, I *do* have control.

With a quiet breath, I yank my power back in. Slowly, the heat slips away. The threat of fire disappears. The other enforcers simmer down.

"—won't make a decision today though we all know this is highly unusual," the justiciar says, continuing a sentence I didn't hear the beginning of.

Okay. Pay attention. This is important.

On the other side of the courtroom, Mai and her sister sit tensely with their eyes straight ahead. The other Redstones calmly watch the judge. Like this is all going just as they planned.

Justice is not for sale among us. That's the main reason enforcers are above the jurisdiction of Families, no matter the level of their power. But maybe justice had not found the right price until now.

The urge to murder flares through me again, a pulse of fire under my skin. But I'm ready for it and easily wrestle it into submission. If the justiciar eventually rules for release, I'll just catch Redstone again. Then kill him before anyone can think of dragging him in front of another court.

The rest of the hearing passes by in a blur of anger. When the justiciar calls for the prisoner to be led away, I signal to one of the others to do it. If I touch him, I won't let him go in one piece.

"This isn't what we do." Nuala, one of the enforcers who was there that day and saw what Ethan had done to Mai, walks quietly at my side as we leave the courtroom. Enforcers walk out before anyone else so we can't be followed and our identities discovered.

Denali, who is based in Atlanta and has worked closely with Mai as Mercy, looks as angry as I feel. "Don't think this is a regular occurrence, Commander," he says to me. "Nuala is right. In our territory, the guilty always get punished."

Ty, the third member of their team, walks with us but says nothing.

"I doubt anyone as powerful as a Redstone has been caught doing something like this. The entire community of Metas is watching to see how we handle the situation." My words are the height of rationality. They don't hint at how much I want to tear Ethan Redstone apart then go after the rest of his corrupt family.

"You're right, Commander," Nuala says. "If we handle this the wrong way then all the ones we've kept in check with our reputation and strength will feel free to do whatever they want and to whoever they want, Meta or human." Her eyes flit minutely from side to side, like she's mentally scrolling through a list of Metas she knows personally who will react just in that way once they feel let off the leash.

I have a list myself, and although it's not long, even a halfway powerful Meta who thinks they can get away with anything is more dangerous than I want to think about.

Damn Mandaia Redstone. She's sacrificing her own child and the safety of the Meta community. How can she live with herself doing something like this?

"We can't let this happen," Denali says. A wave of his hand opens a rippling field of space—our gateway from the hearing and to the enforcer headquarters in Atlanta.

The familiar icy feeling of teleporting comes over me for just a few breaths before we are in the closed Atlanta office belonging to Denali and the enforcers on his team. Ty and Nuala step through the portal with me.

"What he was trying to do to Mai Redstone... Fuck!" Nuala rips off her face covering and stuffs it into her belt. "I don't know why she didn't just kill him then and there. She obviously has the power."

"It's harder killing family than you think," I tell her dryly. Although I'm sure if I hadn't been there to stop Mai that day, she'd have torn her cousin to pieces and not been the least bit sorry.

Nuala makes a rough sound and turns away. The other two take their masks off, a silent show of trust. We only hide our real faces from non-enforcers. I've been short on trust for years now, so I only remove the sleek balaclava-style mask. I keep on the other mask that looks like a human face, close to mine but so far from it that they wouldn't know the real me if I bumped into them on the street. Mai knows me. My aunts know me. And my own enforcer team. That's all.

I don't miss the looks of surprise from the three enforcers, first at me then at each other, when I keep my real face covered.

"We need a plan in case the justiciars let Redstone go," Nuala says after chewing on air for a few minutes.

I cross my arms, watching her steadily. "What do you mean?" Although I'm pretty sure it's clear to all of us what she's suggesting.

Sure, I have my own plan, but they don't need to know that.

"He can't go free. That's not an option. I didn't give up years of my life to train as an enforcer and keep Metas safe just to let this piece of shit loose." Hand fisted, she turns to face us all. "He'll kill again. And the next time he'll be smarter about it so he won't get caught. It won't be long before we start finding more Absolution victims."

No lies there. Well, except for the last part.

With all the vigilante talk, this is getting to be a little too much like a club meeting. Before Nuala starts suggesting we gang up to do something stupid like meet privately later to propose next steps, I clear my throat. "Since I'm the visiting out-of-towner here, I'll say this is my cue to leave. You all do what you like, but I need to check in with my chief and let him know the justiciar decision about Redstone."

"That so-called decision is so off the wall that I'm sure he already knows," Ty says, and it's the first time I hear him speak. His voice is a hoarse rasp, a ruin.

As wound up as he is, he's not stupid enough to confront me. More than my higher rank, his ignorance about what power I have keeps him in check.

"You may be right, Ty, but I'd rather my chief find out from me just the same." With both masks back on, I give them a quick salute and head for the door, already thinking about Mai and the devastation pouring out of her like tears in that hearing. I have to go to her. "Have a good afternoon, all."

"Isn't she supposed to be some kind of badass?" the idiot snarls anyway, just after I close the door behind me. "She shouldn't be afraid to go after some real justice off the books."

"None of us knows what she is, so you better watch yourself," Nuala says, although she sounds as frustrated as her teammate.

She's not wrong.

CHAPTER 11

As soon as I step outside the door and leave the other enforcer team behind, I port away using my own sluggish but effective enough power. Although I took an Uber to the enforcer building to meet Denali and the others, there isn't an ounce of patience left in me to endure that slow means of human transport again. Not when anger and helplessness roils under my skin like this.

Once in Mai's living room, I allow myself a relieved sigh even though my belly is locked in the icy cage that the act of porting clamps around me. Only then do I take off my mask, my gloves. Releasing another sigh, I rub a hand over my naked face. The familiar planes of bone and muscle clothed in skin help me settle into my skin again. Slowly, the anger bleeds away.

The reality of my life, though, stubbornly remains.

Late-afternoon sun drapes the room in gold. The sofa with the blanket I had draped over my lap only a few hours ago. The large blue-and-mink rug where Mai and I wrestled last night when I tried to distract her from the upcoming hearing. Small parts of the home she invited me to share with her. Despite the clear illumination of the sun, this room—this life—feels blurred and insubstantial, on the verge of slipping away.

My knees tremble and lock up.

This situation with Ethan Redstone is only going to get worse. Mandaia Redstone has gone way past words thrown around at a dinner table to actively defending this piece of shit. The wrongness of it pricks tears at the corners of my eyes.

Mandaia's defense isn't only about upping the chance that Ethan will get free. It also means a sharpening of the betrayal Mai must feel.

Shit... The look on her face when Mandaia stood up. Mai's pain seeped into the air then, leaving a bitterness at the back of my throat. The burn of anger on behalf of Mai. Every word Mandaia spoke in support of Ethan was like a physical blow against her daughter.

Mothers are supposed to protect their children, not do...this.

My neck pops when I roll it from side to side to get rid of some of its tension.

Mai needs to be cared for.

A hot bath. Maybe dinner. Takeout from her favorite French restaurant.

Yes, that's what I'll do for her when she gets back.

Decision made, I head for the bedroom. There, I discard my boots and socks and toss my gloves in the small basket meant for parts of my uniform, all the while contemplating what else to do for her. I'm not sure anything can soothe that wounded look I saw on her face across the courtroom. That wound is deep. All I can do now is prevent it from becoming the kind that gets infected and completely breaks down the body.

A quiver in the atmosphere warns me a millisecond before a voice drags me back to the moment.

"Are you fucking kidding me?"

I whirl around, heat quickly gathered in my clenched fists.

Pascale. The breath leaves me in a hiss.

He stands there in normal clothes, jeans and a T-shirt, a light leather jacket over his broad shoulders. His sharp eyes dart around the bedroom, obviously spotting the photo of Mai and me that she insisted on putting on the bedside table next to the one of her and Abi, both wearing identical smiles of happiness.

My limbs turn to ice, but I release the dangerous heat in my fists, lower my hands. "Pascale." I greet him with a nod, playing it cool. "What are you doing here?"

There's no denying where I am. I'm in Mai's bedroom, obviously comfortable enough to take off my masks and my boots. Nothing about this looks like an enforcer paying a professional visit.

"What am I—?" He sputters, words coming to a halt before starting up again. "I followed your signature here and made sure you were alone before I—" Once again, Pascale's words fall away. His eyes blaze with a thousand questions. "This is nuts! Are you—are you fucking Mai Redstone? Her sister? Both of th—?"

"Hell no!" I interrupt before he can make any more crazy guesses. The idea of bedding young Abi makes me all sorts of uncomfortable, like ants crawling across my eyeballs. She's Mai's sister, and that's enough to make her a sister to me, too. "I mean, I'm fucking Mai, yes. Not—not the other one."

Before I even finish talking, he turns away from me, cursing. "Commander...I don't— Do you know how crazy this is?"

Well, I do and I don't.

When I first saw Mai and wanted her, nothing else mattered. As suspicious as I was of her family and as much as I wanted to convince myself that I only seduced her to get close to her and keep her off guard, the truth of it was I started falling for her the moment she opened her mouth and said my name. My jaw aches from its clench.

"Let's talk about this someplace else." I don't want to talk about it at all, but more so, I don't want Mai to come home to this confrontation between me and Pascale. With jerking movements, I pull back on my boots and socks, my gloves.

"Uh...yeah, sure." His pale eyes are a whirling mixture of confusion and betrayal. He holds out a hand and, without hesitation, I take it.

The expected chill of porting comes, washing over me and shuddering away my heat. We appear in the dark. A familiar smell penetrates my nose. A different kind of cold brushes over my face.

Giving him a grunt of approval at his choice of meeting place, I feel along the wall for the light switch. A sharp click illuminates the low-ceilinged room, the tightly packed wall of waist-high human bones along the four walls. Five low wooden stools sit in a circle around a matching table. An iron gate and a black-out curtain stand between us and the single entrance. Pascale's bald head gleams under the low light.

We're almost seventy feet below Paris, surrounded by the city's ancient dead and tucked away in one of the secret tunnels under the city that make up the catacombs, one of the most popular tourist attractions in the city. This room, along with the tunnels leading to and from it, aren't on any of the official maps. We prefer it that way.

Pascale flips up the collar of his jacket in flimsy protection against the damp, subterranean chill. "What's going on, Xóchitl?" Before I get the chance to say anything, he barrels on. "You know this doesn't look good, right?"

Because I wasn't born yesterday, he's not saying anything I don't expect. "I don't care how it looks, I'm in love with Mai Redstone and I'm not letting her go." How's that for honesty?

"Shit!" His eyes widen. "It's like that?"

He curses again and makes a full circuit of the underground room, the heels of his leather boots nearly silent on the limestone floor. When he finally stops, his mouth is tight. Pascale jams his hands into his pants pockets. "Who knows about this?"

"My tias. You. Mai's family. But they don't know I'm an enforcer."

"Jesus… You never make things easy, do you?"

"Not on purpose. This thing with Mai just…happened."

"Knowing you, that's not exactly true. Did you track her down because of Stephen Redstone?"

My cheeks flush with furious heat. Our team works so closely together that we don't keep secrets from each other. Especially not dangerous ones.

When Ixchel was killed, I lived in a constant state of murderous rage, and the team knew it. At first, they tried to soothe me, but once I started talking about the Redstones and my suspicion about what Stephen and Ethan were up to, they encouraged me to deal with the situation then come back to work in a more rational frame of mind.

I did, and then I did.

Although Pascale, Farr, and Caleb don't know I'm the Absolution Killer, they've accepted everything else about me. I have their loyalty and trust, just like they (mostly) have mine. What I found with Mai just felt too...tender to share with them. Or maybe I was just too scared of what they'd think.

"Yes." I finally answer Pascale's question with a slither of regret in my belly. "In the beginning, I did use Mai to get to her family."

Though I didn't know it at the time, Mai deserves more than to be the pawn in a game started by her uncle.

"How did it happen?" Pascale asks.

Because he deserves the real answer, I spill everything that's happened between me and Mai and her family since the start of my hunt for Stephen Redstone.

When I'm done, he looks at me like I've lost my mind. "I'm shocked she's still with you. Then again, I never claimed to understand women."

"Some days, I'm surprised, too." A rusty chuckle tumbles from my mouth. The sound echoes in the partially enclosed tomb.

Pascale shakes his head and gives a weak laugh of his own. He drops down heavily into one of the stools, stretching out his long legs in front of him. Silence presses in on us for endless minutes, and then he says, "You know you have to tell the rest of the team about you and Mai, right?"

He's right. He and the others deserve to know.

"Yes." The inevitability of it tightens my chest, but I swallow my nervousness and face what I need to do like a grown-ass woman. "And there's no time like the present."

CHAPTER 12

MY ONLY CLASS TODAY STARTS long after Mai's first one, but as usual, we decide to arrive at the university together. Save gas and all that even though we weren't too intent on being environmentally conscious in the shower barely an hour ago.

The temptation to have her was too much to resist. The water was cold by the time we stumbled out, breathless and staring anxiously at the clock since her class was due to start in a few minutes. But we made it on time. Even if we both look a little rushed.

Well, I like to think that Mai seems absolutely ravished from our shower romp that almost drowned me, but the truth of it is she looks perfect—intimidatingly gorgeous in cuffed pants and the lavender silk blouse shimmering against her skin.

In my usual pale colors, a gray jumpsuit this time, and with one of her pretty green scarves draped around in my neck, I just look like I got dressed.

"You have some lipstick right there..." Smiling with an evil flash of teeth, she leans toward me and wipes my chin with her thumb. Her thumb comes away with her darker shade. Mai looks smug.

Normally, I wouldn't allow something like that. After all, we're supposed to be discreet whenever we get to campus. Off campus is a whole other story. I'd go down on her in the Starbucks parking lot if she let me.

Scowling, I wipe at my chin, too. "Is there any left?"

"You're fine," she says with another flash of evil. "No one will ever know you just had your face between my legs barely half an hour ago."

"It was fifteen minutes, thank you very much." Yes, we were already running late, but I like to take my time and make sure she comes before I take my own pleasure. Just kissing her some days is enough to make me explode. If I didn't take care of her first, Lord knows when she'd ever get a turn.

She laughs. "As if you'd ever leave me unsatisfied."

It's good to be appreciated.

Smiling wide enough for my face to hurt, I sneak a quick squeeze of Mai's hand.

After three days, the violent ripples from Ethan Redstone's hearing are finally fading away. The bruise in Mai's gaze has hardened into some type of acceptance: this is her family's way and that's it. As for me, when I told Caleb and Farr about my relationship with the Redstone heir, the world didn't end.

Okay, so Farr laughed and called me an idiot while Caleb stared at me like I stole the Holy Grail and have been using it as a water glass the whole time. But at the end of it, they just asked me how secret my relationship was (if the boss asked them about it, should they deny knowing?) and did I plan to go to the next Conclave as Mai's plus one. The answer to both questions was a solid "no."

Two pairs of high heels, mine and Mai's, click against concrete as we cross the courtyard side by side.

The campus is huge. Mammoth buildings with rich people's names on them stretch up toward the sky in a good attempt at being impressive. It's the first day back at school after a long weekend, and I can't wait to get her off campus and back into bed again. Or at least off campus so we can keep enjoying each other without worrying about the anti-fraternization rules.

Enforcing is easier than this. At least there, we have the one rule: Justice above all. Everything else, we can do as we want. It works for me, and it works for the other enforcers.

I refuse to think about the Ethan Redstone farce looming over all of us.

It's crowded today. It's the week before exams start, when everyone who gives a damn is eager to get in the last bit of studying, cheating, or whatever before they sit down to sweat in front of impossible questions.

"Thanks for the clean-up." I purse my lips in her direction. A long-distance kiss. "I'm sure your boss appreciates your efforts to make it look as though we weren't just making out in your car."

"If she knew, I'm sure she would be appropriately thankful."

She probably wouldn't care, though. Mai is one of the best at what she does. Her students love her, and more than one student has come to this school and this campus because of her at the recommendation of a friend or sibling. She is a jewel in the university's crown. They would be stupid to let rules pertaining to grown adults make them shoot themselves in the foot. Then again, no one has ever accused school administrators of being smart.

"Lunch again this afternoon after class?" I ask.

"Can't. One of my students has a small pre-exam crisis and asked me to block off a big chunk of time for her this afternoon. I'll probably end up eating a sandwich and commiserating with her in my office."

If I were anywhere near as dedicated as she is, I'd have the same problem. But the few students I have would rather go to any other professor but me. I'm fine with that. This isn't the job I have the most stake in. "After school, then?"

"Yes. After school." Her lips curve up, and she licks the corner of her mouth just to tease.

"You're not a very nice woman," I say, and turn toward my office. Her class starts soon, but I can just go to my office and get a few things done before my own starts in roughly two hours. The things I do for love. Or after a really fantastic session of shower sex.

A high-pitched scream yanks my attention from the pout of Mai's lips. *What the hell?* What kind of drama are these kids cooking up first thing in the morning? But just as that thought runs through my mind, the emotions behind it hit me.

Fear. Bone-deep terror.

"He's got a gun!" someone shrieks just as the sound of a bullet rockets through the air.

Chaos breaks loose all around us.

Kids are running. Feet pound against the pavement. The formerly orderly campus turns into the scene of a stampede. Someone rushes past me and bumps into my shoulder. They stumble instead of the other way around.

"Mai—" But she's already gone. Briefcase dropped to the ground and disappeared into the madness to do something stupid. Like bring Mercy out of hiding at the place where she damn well works.

I scan the minds around me and feel their terror, the fear that has some of them frozen stupid and others running for their lives. Not far away, the sound of honking horns. Tires screeching. A bump. Some idiot must have run into the street.

Everyone is frightened, but none one can seem to pinpoint where the—*Oh, there he is.*

High up in one of the buildings, a slight boy with a pale face and a long gun peers down from a barely opened window. I feel Mai's presence. Mercy's presence. She's looking but can't find him.

The single-minded purpose of the boy sits like poison in his brain. And his scorn. A torrent of thoughts that have nothing to do with reality and everything to do with his inferiority complex and— what?—a girl didn't want to go out with him? Complete idiocy.

I slip into Mai's head and feed her the boy's location. But she's busy. A student is badly hurt.

Pushing through the screaming crowd, I reach a corner with relatively little chaos and look up to watch the pale boy with the dark gun, staring down into the plaza and getting ready to squeeze off a blaze of bullets. He's only shot one so far, and he's psyching himself up to unload them all.

Why did this have to happen here where we work? There's got to be some sort of rule about this. This should happen at some out-of-the-way place with ill-prepared cops and a slew of politicians waiting to offer thoughts and prayers, but not here where Mercy, damn it, *Mai*, with her superhero complex can get into trouble and nearly get herself killed playing Superwoman.

Damn it.

My heart is pounding fast. But it's not for these humans, it's for Mai. These are bullets, and just a moment of inattentiveness can turn this easy situation into a nightmare.

I curse again and drop my bag along with Mai's briefcase in the corner out of the way so none of the running horde will trip over them. Unlike Mai, I can't easily disguise myself, and though this job means more to her than it does to me, losing it because I show up to play enforcer with my face exposed won't do a damn thing for either of us.

Maybe I should start packing my enforcer uniform for work at the university, too.

At least I'm wearing pants today. Grumbling about the annoying behavior patterns of women with hero complexes, I kick off my high heels and leave them in the same corner as my bag. Then I tie Mai's scarf around the lower half of my face and run through the crowd, toward the danger instead of away from it.

I hope to hell the cameras don't catch me doing something stupid. Or at least something I can't erase later.

"Mai!" Then I catch myself. She needs to focus on her own stupidity, not mine.

I search for that barrage of thoughts again and quickly find the boy. He's moved up to a higher floor. Shots explode from the gun. The bullets are raining down fast, and I fling up my power, overheating the rounds and exploding them just above people's heads before they get the chance to do any damage. I move quickly, shoving the humans out of the way, destroying as many bullets as I can, and running full out for the building with the stupid boy who ruined my damn day. If I catch him before Mai or any of the human police, I'm going to burn that little prick's insides to ashes and laugh while doing it.

I sprint through the building's open doors and to the stairs, not even thinking about the elevator. This building is too damn big. Whimpers of fear reach me. The coppery spill of blood. Adrenaline. Triumph.

My legs stretch and eat up the space between me and boy. Mai is already high up in the building. The sound of bullets has stopped. All I hear now are the cries of terror. Genderless wails of fear.

Just in case Mai isn't as good as she thinks she is, I run faster.

Her mind is calm, though. As always in her crazy moments of heroism, all she's thinking about is who to save. My stomach twists with anxiety, and I almost hate her at that moment.

I'm not someone who feels anxious. Ever.

But I breathe through the unfamiliar emotion, then sweep Mai's thoughts again. She's clear-headed and calm, ready to take on anything that she finds.

Although she's looking, she hasn't found the boy. He's here, though. Hiding. Waiting.

Wait. There he is. The boy. The tip of his long gun is sweeping toward Mai.

"No!" I shout, and the sound roars through me, through the building, and it feels like they hear it all the way in hell. The boy jerks and his gun fires wide. Panic flares in his brain and he takes off, up the stairwell and away from Mai.

She chases him, the breath punching out of her lungs in desperation for him not to hurt anyone else. He's fast. Determined.

So is she.

Call the police, she sends at me as she runs.

I'm pretty sure someone else has taken care of that, I respond, and hear clearly enough for both of us the wail of nearby sirens.

Rescue has arrived. Right.

The boy is pelting up the steps like he's after salvation. Heaven's so close he's practically blinded by it. But Mai is on his trail. Fast and fleet, a gazelle who can break him like a pretzel if she feels like it.

She'll catch him. I slow down and grip the banister to the industrial stairs. This ridiculous thing is almost over.

A scream bursts out. A human girl. A student.

Christ. Please don't let that be someone from one of Mai's classes. She'll be destroyed. With a curse, I throw myself up the stairs and in the direction of the screams. But when I get there, it's not anyone I've ever seen with Mai.

A girl lies slumped over in the stairs. Blood lurid on her sunshine-yellow T-shirt. Whimpers of pain tremble her mouth, and her eyes are wide with fear.

The boy runs up and up and brings his gun up, spraying bullets behind him, but Mai stops for the girl. "Get him!" Mai shouts, gently pressing a hand over the girl's stomach to stop the river of blood.

Get him? That I can do.

I leap forward, the scarf fluttering around my face as I head higher, chasing the boy. Should I teleport? The thought comes as fast as the action, and moments later I'm in front of the boy. His bright green eyes widen. Fear twists his face, and the pleasure of it makes me want to howl.

"Leave me alone!" he shouts as if he has a prayer of me listening to a word he says, but I'm not in the mood for his shit.

My day was god-damn amazing until this idiot screwed everything up. Snarling, I grab the gun and twist it from his hands.

It's hot from all its hard and deadly work, and I rip the magazine from the gun, break the weapon in two, and throw the pieces behind me. They clatter down the stairs toward Mai with the wounded girl. Screaming more words I don't have the patience for, the boy flings himself at me.

"You little shit." I punch him, and he sails back. His body flies toward the window. And out. Glass breaking. The rag doll of him explodes out into the brilliance of the morning, the look on his face of comic dismay. Right. He didn't think it would end like this.

Screams rise up from below.

I don't wait to hear the thump of his body on the pavement. Mai is more important.

My mind searches for her and immediately finds what it needs. Mai is with the wounded girl in a too-slow elevator. The girl's eyes are glassy from pain and fear. Blood bubbles out of her perforated belly, and Mai holds on to her tight. She's called an ambulance to have them waiting for them when she gets to the bottom floor.

The threat is gone.

Slowly, my breath calms. My anger at the boy bleeds away.

The sounds of sirens and cries of pain and more rush in through the broken window. A police radio squawks with noise and mysterious numbers and call signs I never bothered to learn. Everything inside me begins to still. Then panic. The fear for Mai. The burst of anger that threw my fist harder than necessary at that human boy.

My legs shake, barely keeping me upright in the middle of the hallway. The cloth over my mouth flutters with every breath I take. Cameras. I feel them on me. But at least my face is covered. Still, I'll have Farr wipe any footage of me. This isn't official enforcer business, but I can use the excuse of keeping my identity secret as a reason to interfere with the human's technology.

Humans.

Mai.

The dead boy ten stories below.

I squeeze my eyes shut imagining Mai's face when she sees the boy's crushed body and realizes I am the reason for it. The contentment from this morning seems so very far away now. Like it existed in another world. Slowly, I open my eyes and prepare to face the consequences of this one.

CHAPTER 13

THEY SHUT DOWN THE UNIVERSITY. But not before I grab my bag, Mai's briefcase, and my shoes, and escape from the chaos-ridden campus. Human police are everywhere. News helicopters circle above the sadness and blood, and reporters hustle close, pushing at the cordoned-off scene to feast on firsthand details of this latest mass shooting. I'm too weakened from teleporting with the boy killer to do anything other than slip through side streets, trying not to look suspicious.

I find Mai at home.

She stands as herself, Mercy costume discarded in favor of jeans and a well-worn T-shirt, in the living room like she's waiting for me. Her face is a storm of misery and anger. "Why did you kill him?"

It's the question I expected, but I thought she'd at least ask if I'm okay first. My bag and Mai's land on the sofa. My shoes tumble into a corner by the front door. I'm drained and a little irritated, immediately put on the defensive.

"He killed at least three of your precious humans, and he would have killed more if you hadn't stopped him."

Mai growls and stalks toward me. "You mean if *you* hadn't stopped him." She stops only a few inches from me, so close I can feel her breath on my face. Her anger blazes high enough to rival any of my fires. "I saw you." Her eyes are narrow and black. "I saw you take out those bullets before they even hit." There is accusation in those eyes, and pain. "You could've made his gun explode then and stop things from being as they did." She drew in a long and shuddering breath. "Why didn't you save them?"

"Oh, could I? You know so much about my power, do you?" I growl back at her, unable to stem the tide of anger rising up out of my exhaustion. "I bet you know mine about as well as you know yours." She could've been killed running around after this kid with just about unlimited bullets for his gun and the lack of fucks when it came to using them.

I lingered enough to hear that the kid's father was in the army. He stole the rifle from him. Brought his small penis to school, backed up by a big gun, and hoped to take out as many of his classmates as possible, including the girl who didn't want him.

None of this is my fault, and the nerve of her to say this makes me want to shake her. "You're the one running around playing hero, Mai. Not me. My job is to take out Metas who kill or abuse other Metas. I don't protect humans. But today, I did. For you."

Her arms cross tightly over her chest. "But you could've saved them all if you wanted to."

"That's bullshit and you know it."

Sadness leaks from her like her tears. She's shaking. Mercy's red half-mask bursts to the surface of her face, then disappears. Skin the color and hardness of a turtle's shell morphs over her throat. Sharp, dagger-like spikes erupt from her forearms before melting away. Her skin ripples with change after change, one right after another. All her control is gone.

The human girl must be dead.

I risk a look into her mind, and it says how pissed I am that I'm not as precise as usual, or as careful. She winces at my clumsy mental probe and jerks wounded eyes up at me. The deep red of the Mercy mask slips over her features, then falls away in the next breath. Talons appear in place of her fingernails.

"Stay out of my head!"

I feel a push, then abruptly nothing. None of my Mai's thoughts. None of her feelings. She's a blank wall to me, as if I never loved her. A gasp spills out of me.

How did she do that, and why?

My feet take a single, stumbling step toward Mai. "What did you just d—?"

She jerks two steps back and confronts me with the flat gold of her eyes. "Yes, she's dead." Her voice is a low growl, half-transformed into something bestial. "And you could've stopped that, too."

The blank wall where the cool ripple of her thoughts and feelings used to be twists my stomach with dread and fear. Like someone has suddenly taken away the safety net from beneath the trapeze of my life.

Doubt. Fear. Uncertainty. Things that were unknown between us now grip me in a merciless vice.

Although I am frozen on the inside, my mouth runs away from me, propelled by the pain breaking me into little pieces.

"No." A snarl of self-defense twists my lips. "I will not take responsibility for that. You run around this city in a costume trying to save every human from themselves and each other, not for once accepting you're fighting a losing battle. That battle isn't one I'm fighting. It's not one I've chosen. Do not put that burden on me."

A spasm of pain wracks her face, and she spins away from me. "I can't…I can't look at you right now. Just…"

"Just what?" I can already taste the bitter poison of the words waiting on the edge of her tongue. "What exactly do you want me to do, *Mandaia-Pili*?"

Say it. Although Mai isn't listening anymore, I force my thoughts at her, daring her to finish her slow annihilation of me.

Although I can only see the side of her face now, the flinch jerks her whole body. "You always know just how to twist the knife, don't you?" Fresh tears pour down her cheeks to wet the fabric of her T-shirt. As if she isn't the one who started this. "Out of the two of us, *you* are the one who's like my mother." Then she turns and walks away, heading for her bedroom where I always felt welcome before. But not now.

Her back is iron. Everything about her posture says "Don't follow. Stay away."

All because of the fear I felt for her and the useless anger of some puny human who felt mighty with his gun. I turn. I grab my things and leave. The hurt is hard to swallow, but I do it.

The elevator takes forever to arrive and then, stuck inside, it leaves me staring at my stone-faced reflection for longer than I can bear.

A muscle tics in my jaw.

My eyes look black.

The hole inside me where Mai has yanked herself loose throbs like an open wound.

Six floors and dozens of heartbeats later, I finally reach the lobby and do my best not to stumble out into the too-bright sun like someone with no center to keep them upright.

Then the back of my neck prickles.

Someone is *watching* me. The alien gaze burns into my back and the side of my face like acid. *Who the fuck…?*

My head jerks up and I look around, nostrils flaring, my hunter senses spreading out to catch the scent. A familiar and comforting rage roars in me, and I welcome this transformation of my pain. My hands burn hot with the lust to burn everything to ground. To hollow out the bastard daring to watch me like I'm some self-destructing beast for their entertainment and later dissection.

There! A pulse of color, a hint of an unknown spice in the air. Another Meta.

Without conscious thought, my body bursts into motion, darting in the direction of my stalker.

When I find you, whoever you are, I'll burn you from the inside out and make you wish you'd never set eyes on me. I'll rip the screams out of you. Your carcass will bleed.

My feet fly across the pavement. I feel heat trail in my wake. The streets aren't empty, but I don't care. Let the humans stare and scurry out of my way. Let them see me in a way Mai doesn't.

My feet stumble.

Sudden tears blind me, and I'm running through a veil of wet, tracking a Meta signature I can barely see through my pain. I race through a maze of buildings on a side street, down a sloping avenue. The signature of my prey abruptly changes, and I turn to chase it. And slam into the side of a building. Bricks explode around my body. Dust from the impact billows up and I choke, sobbing out a cry. A scream of frustration.

"Come back here!" But they're gone.

Fuck.

Humans are watching; some have their cell phones pointed at me. Double fuck.

The broken wall shudders as I drop back against it, my insides dirty with hurt and my breath heaving. All this effort for nothing.

I swallow to try and catch my breath, but it feels like the hardest thing I've ever done. The broken wall digs into my back through my clothes. Shivers click my teeth. Like the bricks at my feet, I'm crumbled to pieces and only Mai can put me back together again.

But will she?

CHAPTER 14

IT'S BEEN TWO DAYS, AND Mai has not come back to me.

Technically, *I* haven't gone back to her apartment, but from the way she's kept her mind firmly closed to me, it feels like she doesn't want me there. She hasn't whispered a single word through the bond we're supposed to have. It hurts.

While huddled in my overpriced room at the Ritz, I thought over and over again about what happened at the school, about my argument with Mai afterward, and then my later stupidity. At least I had the presence of mind to ask Farr and Caleb to scrub any digital and mental records of my lunatic sprint through Mai's neighborhood. But that was as far as my clear thinking went.

My thoughts were otherwise rabid but didn't change a damn thing.

Which is why I've decided to search for her the human way.

Pushing aside my feelings of humiliation, I open the door of the classroom where she's supposed to be.

Of course, Mai isn't here.

The room isn't empty, though. Three of her students linger, their belongings packed away but their bodies draped across chairs in the back of the classroom like they're in no hurry to leave. There's not another class scheduled to be here for another two hours.

"—and that skank Elisa was telling everyone who would listen that Professor Redstone is sleeping with one of her students. Basically implying that she's the one munching on the prof's muff after hours." One of the students, a thin boy with a bright pink undercut, makes the bold statement. He's sitting on top of one of the desks, his profile to the door, obviously irritated.

A mischievous-looking girl in cut-off shorts and a Black Lives Matter T-shirt laughs as though what the boy says is comedy gold. "As if."

"Right! I wish the prof was down to fuck one of us. I'd be the first one in line." This comes from Beatrice Aarondale, a student of Mai's who I stupidly thought she was screwing before we met. "But everyone knows she doesn't get down like that. Sadly." She sags across her desk in a belted dress short enough to be a shirt.

"What does that even mean?" The boy makes a sound of annoyance and waves his hand in truly dramatic fashion. His swoosh of pink hair falls over one eye in his agitation. "Professors sleep with students around here all the time and nobody ever gets busted for it. It's like there's some kind of Scout badge to screw your prof and blog about it. They don't have a shit ton of student/teacher porn out there for nothing."

"True," Cut-off says.

The door of the classroom opens and then falls shut behind me as someone peeks in. It makes a soft, squeaking noise, bringing an end to my accidental eavesdropping.

Beatrice sits up from her slouch and narrows her eyes at me. I don't have to read her mind to know what she's thinking.

"Are you the one who started those stupid rumors?" she asks me.

This girl has a set of ovaries on her. If I didn't know for sure that my woman doesn't want her, I'd be tempted to rip her apart with words alone. But her obsession with Mai is completely one-sided, and Mai has let her know that more than once. Beatrice's loyalty to my woman in the face of this personal rejection is one of the sweetest things I've seen from a human in a long time.

It doesn't mean I'll allow her to come for me, though.

I fix Beatrice with a cool stare. "Why would I start rumors when I'm the one who has the pleasure of munching on her muff after hours?"

Why did I just say that? Because I'm apparently a jealous idiot.

The boy lets loose a dramatic gasp, and his other friend's mouth drops open. Beatrice looks like she wants to kill me with her bare hands and then piss on my cooling body.

"You're lying," she finally growls. Her eyes narrow to slits, and her arms cross tight under her breasts. The little trouble-maker knows I'm not lying, though.

"Of course." I make my smile as insincere as possible. "If you happen to see Professor Redstone, will you tell her I'm looking for her, please?" Since Beatrice would rather see me under a literal bus than tell Mai anything on my behalf, I make sure to aim the request at her friends.

Beatrice makes a rude noise. "If you're sleeping with her, shouldn't you know where she is? Or at least have her phone number and oh, I dunno, communicate with her like normal girlfriends?"

Okay, I take back every good thing I ever thought about this girl.

"Normal is relative, as I'm sure you very well know, Ms. Aarondale." I give her a look that tells her I know all about her kinks, from mild to wild. "Anyway, thank you for the lovely conversation. I'll leave you all to it."

Just as my hand reaches the door handle, it turns and the door slowly begins to push open. A young-looking girl stumbles through it.

"Oh!"

Pale eyes. Sun-kissed skin. Thick black hair down to her waist. A face full of disappointed expectations.

These impressions come to me in a flash, but I've been enforcing for too long to focus only on what someone looks like in the moment. Being with Mai taught me more of the same. The girl's eyes are wide with surprise, and she reaches out with both hands to stop her fall into me. Turning quickly, I avoid the touch of her hands altogether and grab her by the shoulder to stop her from falling on her face. Her skin is hot to the touch even though the layer of her T-shirt separates her skin from mine.

"Excuse me!" She jumps back from my touch, her side slamming into the wall. "I thought there was a class in here now."

"Professor Redstone canceled it." Beatrice comes up behind me, frowning and curious. "She sent the cancellation notice to all her students last night." She peers at the girl as if Beatrice is the jailbait version of a TV detective. "You don't look familiar. Are you sure you have the right class?"

"I'm not one of hers, at least not yet," the girl says with a smile that's trying a little bit too hard. She toys with her hair, pulling the entire thick length over one shoulder and petting it like a good dog. "I just wanted to check it out before making my mind about taking it next semester." Her eyes don't stop moving around the mostly empty classroom.

Lured by the promise of a bit of drama, the pink-haired boy and his giggling friend move up from the back of the room. Though I'm not trying to listen in on their minds, I sense their curiosity. Their amusement.

With her hands shoved into the pockets of her so-called dress, Beatrice blatantly looks the girl over. "She's not teaching the same thing next semester. The 202-level course is next semester, and that's a continuation of what we're going over now. If you sign up next semester you won't know what's going on."

"Sorry! I didn't know that." The girl jerks her hands from the hypnotic stroking of her hair and lifts them in the air in surrender. Her eyes are big and wide. Aggressively innocent. "Thanks for telling me."

"No problem," Beatrice says, apparently appeased by the girl's apology and submission. "You can just email her and tell her what you're interested in. In regard to her classes, that is."

Behind us, her friends are having a giggling fit.

The byplay between the girls is strangely fascinating. Beatrice is treating the newcomer like she's trespassing. Was I ever this territorial about any professor in college? I hope not.

Anyway, enough of this. I'm not a student to play games when it comes to getting what I want. And I'm certainly not going to guard Mai like a jealous pit bull.

"Excuse me, everyone."

With a pointed step toward the door, I once again wish the students a good afternoon. Mai is out there somewhere with whatever resentment she has still burning in her heart. I need to extinguish it before it completely incinerates this precious thing we have between us.

CHAPTER 15

ESCAPE HAS NEVER BEEN MY thing. When something tries to corner me, I fight to their death to get free. But an escape is exactly what I'm looking for now in Mexico.

Half-dreading the reception my aunts will give me after my weeks of absence, I walk out to the backyard pool after teleporting into the house. Sweat and honeysuckle-scented Caribbean heat immediately prickle under my leather jacket. A breath of relief pours out of me.

I'm home.

"So, we finally get more than a weekly phone call from you." Lying back in her over-sized hammock near the pool, Tia Ana sways back and forth in the light breeze while the sun glints over her tower of silver hair. Sunglasses hide her eyes, but her attitude is on full display. She barely responds to my hug.

"I don't know why you say 'we' since I'm okay with our niece living her own life." Her sister, Carmen, speaks up from her massive rainbow-and-white-unicorn floaty in the middle of the pool. Her short midnight-black hair is wet at the edges. She blows me a kiss and takes a sip from her margarita glass before putting it back in the cupholder built into the floaty. A similar glass, only empty, rests on the floor near Tia Ana's hammock.

With my socks and ankle boots off and jeans rolled halfway up my calves, I drop my leather jacket on the lounge chair next to Ana in her hammock and try to defend myself. "I call you more than once a week."

Tia Ana throws me an unimpressed look but responds to her sister. "I want her to live her own life, but it wouldn't kill her to visit more often. Why have the power to be anyplace in the world if you don't come home?"

"You know my power doesn't work like that." I can teleport just about anywhere I choose, but my use of the power is limited. One shot and I can't use it again for hours. Which is the reason I usually only use it for work.

"Still…" Tia Ana refuses to let it go.

Carmen flicks her fingers in the water toward her sister. "Leave her alone." Then she turns a smile to me. "Anyway, Xóchitl. This one may be set on giving you nothing but tears for visiting, but I for one am glad to see you."

"Thank you, Tia Carmen." I give her floating unicorn a playful nudge with my bare toe.

"If we knew you were coming, we could've made tamales," Tia Ana grumbles. "You don't even allow us to spoil you anymore." Tamales are my favorite, and nobody makes them like my tias.

"We can make some together later if you're in the mood." The tamales take forever to make, but it would help settle my mind to fall into the rhythm of cooking and conversation.

"Later sounds good. Doesn't it, Ana?" But Tia Carmen doesn't wait for her sister to answer. She turns immediately back to me. "How long are you staying?"

Good question. "A couple of days. Three, maybe. Depending."

"Depending on what?" Ana pushes up her glasses to her forehead. Her steady brown gaze would make me confess to murder if she didn't already know everything I've done.

"Depending on how much grief that woman of hers is giving her, obviously." Tia Carmen's smile is far too knowing. She drinks down the last of her margarita and tucks the empty cup back in the cup-holder of her unicorn float.

"Is this crazy sister of mine right?" Tia Carmen asks with a hint of glee. "Are you girls actually breaking up? When Mai was here, you acted like you'd never let her out of your sight again, much less your life."

God. Was I that obvious back then?

The one and only time Mai has been to my house was a few months ago when I asked her to come and think about being my woman. On that weeklong visit, she met my aunts who fed her and told her stories about me they should've kept to themselves. Everyone got along.

Despite the cockiness I showed Mai, I was shocked she took the chance on coming to Mexico to see me. In the time we were apart, I missed her and hoped she missed me, too. With the promise of getting answers to the questions she had about my identity and my reasons for being in Atlanta, I lured her here into my world.

We managed to work everything out between us, and Mai ended up in bed with me that night.

"I don't think we're breaking up," I finally say after a hard swallow. "Mai just needs some space right now and I need..." My throat clicks, and the sudden desire to hide under something dark and cool makes me want to hit something.

"Us. You need us, *cariño*." Tia Carmen regards me gently through the lenses of her pink-tinted sunglasses.

A breath of relief. "Yes, that's exactly what I need." It's a comfort not having to explain.

But Tia Ana isn't done with me. "You left here without once looking over your shoulder. Now abandoning us to go live with a stranger doesn't seem so right, does it?"

"*Dios!* Ease up, Ana. Luz didn't give birth to Xóchitl for her to live her life for us. Xóchitl has to chase her own happiness just like we had the chance to when we were young."

"Chasing her happiness doesn't have to mean running away from us." Tia Ana sits up to stare us both down, and the hammock rocks alarmingly with her sudden movement. "We are the only family she has left. And this girl is what? Another Redstone all set to inherit her mother's crooked empire. When that happens, Mai Redstone will have no time for the love Xóchitl gave us up for."

This is my aunt at her most dramatic, but the truth behind her words slams into me like a sledgehammer. This thing between Mai and me came together quickly and not too long ago. Just three months in and we're already fighting. About her family. About Mercy. About strangers who've tried to kill her.

Does our relationship have any kind of future?

My hair feels rough and dry when I drag my fingers over it. I wish I could destroy all of my aunt's doubts with my own certainty. But how can I when the doubts sound like the same ones rolling around in my own head?

As for the other thing… "I've never forgotten that you're my family, Tia. I'll never forget how important the two of you are to me. I just want something sweet for myself." I'm a breath from pleading for her to understand. The hot lump in my throat slides down then up with my swallow.

Tia Ana makes a dismissive noise. "That Redstone girl is far from sweet."

She doesn't know Mai like I do, though. Maybe that's part of the problem. Just like Mai keeps trying for me to have dinners and whatever else with her family, I probably should make at least a little effort to bring her into mine. My tias have only seen Mai come here, seduce and smile, and take me away. They don't know the look of Mai when she's staying.

Or maybe I don't know the look of her when she's done and halfway out the door.

Shit.

"Okay. That's enough." Tia Carmen's voice snaps through the awkward silence. Her laid-back attitude is gone. "Ana, she loves the girl and she loves us, too. All this is recent. Give her a chance to find her balance and get off her ass. She'll only fall away from us if you keep kicking at her. Don't force her to choose when she doesn't have to."

I roll my shoulders back and stretch my neck to one side and then the other to ease the tight coil of tension in me. It doesn't help.

"Xóchitl, go put on your swimsuit and make us some fresh drinks. I'll calm my sister down in the meantime. The day is too nice for all this drama." She tosses this last bit at Aunt Ana, trailing her fingers through the water. "Go, *cariño*," she says when I don't immediately move.

"Okay, Tia Carmen." A quick look at Tia Ana finds her face soft and already drawn with lines of regret. She gently tilts her head toward the house, and I scramble to my feet for escape.

What is it about these women that turns me into a needy child?

My bedroom glows with sunlight. Everything is just like I left it a few months ago, including the extra set of pajamas folded on top of the storage trunk at the foot of the bed. Seeing Mai wearing my clothes and tugging them off her in the middle of the night is one of the brighter pleasures I remember from the week she was here.

It's a pleasure I might never have again.

No wonder so many people hate relationships. All this uncertainty and fear that comes with them is just pure torture. Only a masochist would deal with this kind of crap over and over again. Naked, I pull out a bikini from the armoire and slip it on without looking at my reflection. There's nothing new to see there.

A half an hour later, I leave the kitchen with a tray of margaritas to replace the nearly empty glasses both women have. As I pass Tia Ana her drink, she grabs my hand and squeezes it. Her eyes are full of apology and love.

"I worry for you, my flower. That's all."

"I know." I clear the roughness from my throat and settle on the stone steps of the pool, a drink in hand. The water is cool where it comes up to my waist but warms quickly.

Looking happily between the two of us, Tia Carmen moves her feet back and forth in the water to steer her floaty. The rainbow unicorn sails toward the center of the pool, and she sips her drink with a hum of satisfaction.

My family.

"So, what did you troublemakers get into while I was gone?" I ask.

Carmen snorts delicately. "You're the only trouble, *cariño*."

My favorite aunt climbs from her hammock carefully holding her margarita. "It's the usual routine around here. Nothing exciting."

Her feet hit the water with a mild splash, and with her ornate twist of silver hair far above the water and her drink in one hand, she swims toward me. "We like the quiet." Dripping wet from the shoulders down, she settles on the steps next to me with her margarita.

My mother, their sister, was an enforcer. Her power had been tremendous: flight and weather manipulation. She'd also been terrifying beautiful.

My tias used to joke that the gods unfairly gave their sister all the real power when it should have been spread among all the girls. But my tias never wanted any special power. Unless a Meta is part of an influential family, real power only comes with real problems. No one wanted my mother to be an enforcer, but she jumped at the chance.

And now she is dead, killed in the same "accident" as her husband and one of her sisters.

"A quiet life is nice," I agree.

Although my tias know about my job, I try to keep them as far from it as possible. Outside my small family and the people at work, only Mai knows I'm an enforcer. It's safer that way.

My tia bumps my shoulder. "Quiet is a good thing for you? You don't act like it."

Before I can say anything, Tia Carmen comes to my rescue. "You know she only did those terrible things because of Ixchel." Her voice is low, and the echo of her words momentarily blankets the backyard in a somber silence. None of us have gotten past my sister's death.

Tia Ana is relentless, though. "You should give up the work and just be, Xóchitl. Enjoy the blood rushing through your veins at an even pace instead of fueled by adrenaline and fear for your life."

They always refer to what I do as "the work," never saying "enforcer" out loud in case someone is listening. I've never teased them for their paranoia.

"You know I'd only get bored," I tell them. "There's only so much quiet I can stand without ripping my hair out by the roots and running naked down the streets screaming."

It's only a slight exaggeration.

The acres the house sits on are lush and fertile. My aunts could sell what they grow but instead choose to live off the food and animals, then trade what's leftover with a few select people in the town nearby. They're happy.

"Sometimes I think you only define the quality of your life by the amount of trouble you get into." Carmen floats close to me with her eyes closed and the straw of the margarita between her lips. A light breeze propels her gently across the pool. "There's nothing wrong with that, *cariño*. Your mother was the same way after a while."

The things we get used to.

"I hope it's not the same," I say with a twist to my mouth. "The last thing I want to do is get any of you killed."

A shrug from Tia Ana. "People will do what they will do."

And I'll kill anyone who tries to hurt the ones I love.

Mai drifts to the forefront of my mind again. My belly clenches viciously at the thought of never holding her again. Sometimes it scares me how fast I fell for her. No matter how many fights we have or what happens with us in the future, she's firmly lodged in my heart.

The sound of the doorbell interrupts my thoughts. Ana and Carmen both look up and meet each other's eyes. Something is going on. The twinned thoughts from them overlap, more feeling than anything. Something has been going on since I last left. Carmen reaches for her cell phone tucked into another pocket on her floaty and swipes a few times, calling up an image of the front gate and the cameras capturing every angle of the property.

"Someone from the village," she says, then shoves the phone toward the edge of the pool where Ana can reach it.

Interesting, since the village is at least an hour away by car, a mixture of bumpy and smooth roads. Ana hands me the phone and heads into the house toward the front. She could just walk around the yard and go to the front gate that leads directly to the verandah, but she's being cautious. Why?

I meet Carmen's eyes. "Wait," she tells me.

The image of the front door is on the phone, the empty veranda, shadows of leaves overhead that move in the breeze.

A few seconds later, Ana appears on the screen. She steps off the veranda in a hastily thrown on shift. The sandals on her feet slap gently on the smooth stone path as she heads to our innocuous-looking front gate.

There's nothing overtly secure about our house at first glance. But anyone who arrives at the gate finds no obvious latch to open. They have to ring an electronic bell in the low stone fence to get anyone's attention. An invisible barrier above the fence stops dead anyone who tries to jump over.

Through the camera, a boy waits at the fence. He's a teenager, no more than maybe fifteen years old. I know him, and I know his family.

Ana waves to him. *"Hola, Pablito."*

"Bueñas tardes, Señora."

They go through a round of pleasantries while the boy's eyes roam over the house, veranda, and backyard barely visible through a dense thicket of flowers and fruit trees.

After many minutes, he finally gets to the point of his visit. "Our trees are bursting with pomegranates, and we can barely eat them all. Do you have any tomatoes or corn to trade?" His eyes don't stop moving.

"No tomatoes or corn, Pablito. At least not yet. We should have some mature avocados by the end of the month if you want that."

"You'll be harvesting, then. Will Xóchitl come to help?"

"No. It's just me and Carmen. There's more than enough muscle to go around between me and my sister for such a small crop."

There's more, but I tune them out to question my aunt with a look.

"Strange, right?" She tips her head toward the conversation being captured on the phone's screen.

"What's going on?"

"We're not sure. In the past three weeks or so, a few people have come from the village to barter or buy from us. About eight different requests spread out more or less evenly. Whether or not we have something they want, they always manage to ask about you in some way."

"Three weeks?" Although I try to fight it, icy dread crawls down my spine. "Why didn't you tell me this before?"

"Ana and I were actually going to let you know the next time we talked on the phone. This kind of traffic isn't normal for us."

No kidding.

The conversation at the front gate wraps up, and Pablito climbs into an old pickup truck waiting nearby. My hand is a hard fist at my side. Security cameras perched in the trees capture the image of the pale blue truck turning around on the road to head back to the village instead of moving on toward the other side of the mountain and our nearest neighbor who grows more than we do, sells as well as barters, and probably has what Pablito says he's looking for.

What the hell is going on?

When Ana comes back, I get to my feet. "I can't stay." If people are searching for me here, then they know exactly who they're on the hunt for.

"But you just got here." Carmen shoves her sunglasses to the top of her head. Her eyes are wet with disappointment.

"You watched that boy just like I did. If I stay here, they'll keep bothering you, and then what?" The thought of what could happen to my aunts, my last relatives, the women who raised me and Ixchel once our parents were killed, fills me with a creeping terror. My heart kicks hard against my ribs.

"They were searching for you before you got here," Ana reminds me with a snap in her voice. She stands with her hands on her hips.

"I can't stay," I say again. So much for tamales and comfort. It would be selfish to keep my aunts in the crosshairs of some unknown enemy just because I'm feeling sad.

With a low growl, I shove down the thick lump of fear and disappointment rising in my throat. Someone's out there hunting me. I have to find them first and show them exactly why that's the biggest mistake they ever made.

CHAPTER 16

I didn't say the words.

THE TEXT MESSAGE FROM MAI comes a day after I've been back from Mexico. I nearly tripped over my own feet dashing across the hotel room to grab the phone from where it sits charging on the desk.

I didn't say the words. Come back home, please. We should talk.

Three damn days later. But at least she sent the message. Stupid hope rises up in my chest like an ill-timed burp.

Does she want me to come now?

Automatically, my mind reaches out for hers. Again, nothing. She's cut off my mental access to her as easily as blocking my number from calling her phone. I swallow the hope and accompanying sadness, looking down at the last part of the text. *We should talk.* Nobody in the history of relationships ever wants to hear or see those words.

But I need to see her more than I want to avoid the implied threat.

A quick glance at Mai's online calendar gives me a jolt. She and I have a date.

Is that why she texted me today?

With no room for second-guessing, I mentally rearrange my calendar: Sleep, mope, and sad masturbate until my fingers fall off get moved to tomorrow, and I prep myself for seeing Mai tonight.

Just about worshipped for its reputation for incredible food in a romantic, Old World setting, Pleasure and the Palate regularly makes every best-of-whatever list in the city. In bed one evening after we made love, Mai confessed to a desire to go, but only with a lover. I made the reservation for us the next day.

That was over a month ago.

"Good evening, ma'am." The maître d greets me as I walk up a few minutes early.

On a Friday evening, the restaurant is full, but with the plentiful space between each table, soft lighting, and well-placed furniture, it doesn't feel crowded.

"Good evening." I keep my tone cool to temper my excitement at seeing Mai again. "I'm Xóchitl Bentley. I have a reservation here for two. Redstone and Bentley. Either-or."

In his tailed tuxedo and with surprise on his suspiciously unlined face, he looks like a startled penguin. He glances briefly over his shoulder before consulting a book on the podium in front of him.

"There might be some sort of misunderstanding," he says after a few awkward moments scanning the large, hardbound ledger. "I have it here that the Bentley party is already at the table and nearly a half an hour into the meal."

Surprise makes my voice sharp. "A half an hour? Doubt it. I'm a little early for our eight o'clock reservation."

The man darts a gaze behind me at what is probably a growing line. I don't bother looking.

His hands grip the sides of the podium. The politeness is seconds away from sliding off his face. "According to our records, someone called to move the reservation up by half an hour. Your party arrived and is currently on the first bottle of wine."

Bottle of wine. That means Mai didn't come here alone. My fingernails dig into my palm. "A bottle of wine is big enough to share. I'll just go over and join them."

"That's not possible, I'm afraid. It's a table for two."

Oh, you're not afraid yet… My anger threatens to bubble up, but I clamp down on my tongue. Hard.

"All right," I speak through the flood of blood over my tongue. "In that case, I'll just go over and see who's been impersonating me these days."

It better not be one of those inferior models Mai dated before me. The anger floods me like super-heated steam. I feel seconds away from blowing all the way up. I'm not jealous, I'm pissed.

The maître d stutters. "I don't think that's a good idea, ma'am."

There are a few ways I can handle this, but I do it the way my Tia Carmen would approve of. My smile comes out to play.

"It'll only be a simple hello…" His name tag gleams gold from his right breast. "Ralph. Nothing at all to worry about. I'll be there and gone in just a few minutes."

The restaurant is busy. He doesn't want a scene, and although it would be entertaining in a few ways, it's not worth it for me to have one, either.

I up the sincerity of my smile and soften my eyes. The man isn't a flutter of butterflies I can charm into doing what I want, but I do my best. "Promise."

It only takes a moment for him to crack completely. I'm sure the growing line behind me doesn't hurt. "Very well." A smile twitches across his face. "I'll have Julie show you to their table."

He lifts a hand, and a woman in a loose black dress and high heels appears as if by magic. "Please show Ms. Bentley to table sixteen."

Julie smiles like a toothpaste model and grabs a menu from beside the podium before Ralph can let her know I'm only going there for a quick visit.

"Come with me, please." Julie turns in a swish of black cotton.

"Of course." I follow the woman, both sets of our high heels tapping against the old-fashioned stone floors of the restaurant. But the sound is mostly swallowed up by the conversations flowing in every corner, the occasional burst of restrained laughter, the low and inoffensive music surrounding us like a tepid bath.

The place has a great ambiance even if the food turns out to be garbage.

Mai and another woman are sitting at what must be one of the best tables in the house. A bit tucked away from everyone else, at a window overlooking the garden of herbs and whatever else pretentious places like this pretended to grow on premises so people can feel good about eating "organic." It's a beautiful set-up though. Even I have to admit that.

The lights from the old-fashioned crystal chandeliers are low and golden, washing over the women, their table with its bottle of wine, a full bread basket, two place settings with patterned china, silver cutlery, and glasses of brilliantly red wine. It looks like a scene like an Italian Renaissance painting.

It should be me sitting at this table with Mai. Not this person.

"Here you are." Julie shows me to the table like she's presenting royalty. At Julie's words, Mai looks up. Her beautiful lips fall open. While Mai is distracted and her dinner companion—my replacement—looks down at her menu, oblivious, Julie slips the menu at the empty space at the table then looks around with confusion.

Three women. A table set for two. Whatever should she do? Julie pulls a smartphone from a clever little pocket in her dress and starts tapping away on the screen.

In the meantime, Mai keeps staring. Appreciation glimmers in her eyes, which is a good thing since I dressed for her. Tonight, for the first time in years, I'm wearing color.

All my life, I've been drawn to neutral shades. Gray, beige, bone. Never white, though. And just about everything in my closet is from that family. But for Mai, just for tonight, to make her truly see me, I've worn something the color of the sun.

The dress is a light gold silk. It clings lightly to my figure but moves easily when I walk. It drapes like an invitation over my bra-less breasts, the loose waist caressing my flat belly with each step, the gold material like water over my hips and thighs. Strappy gold sandals complete the outfit along with a white-gold flower clip in my short curls.

I'm an offering, ready to prostrate myself on the altar of our love.

"Good evening, Mai." I'm pleasant and as nice as can be. There's not even a hint of the burning anger I feel. "How are you? I see you gave away my seat at the table."

She drags her eyes away from me to stare at her dinner companion like she's never seen her before.

It's Caressa. Her cousin from that lovely dinner party with her family a few weeks ago. The same cousin who was at Mandaia's side when she defended Ethan to the justiciar.

Mai fiddles briefly with an earring before clasping her hands in her lap. "I didn't think you'd still want to come, and you know I really wanted to have dinner here. So Caressa volunteered when I was telling her about it the other day."

Did she now? From this cozy setup, Mai seems to have forgiven Caressa's presence at the hearing on Ethan's behalf. Granted, the senator didn't say anything during the witness portion, but where she sat during the entire shit show spoke volumes about who had her loyalty.

Finally, I spare more than a passing look to the cousin. Playing the butch today to Mai's super femme, she wears leather wingtips, a slim-fit suit, and a skinny tie. All in black except for the snow-white dress shirt. Her waist-length hair has been twisted into a sleek French roll, and diamonds wink from the lobe of each ear. Just like the last time I saw her, she is attractive enough in a way that all of us are, but nothing special.

There is *something* about her, though, that suggests she's some kind of mental manipulator and not just a moderately talented empath. Automatically, my mental defenses rise to counteract whatever she may decide to throw at me. Mai may have forgotten where Caressa sat during the hearing, but I haven't.

A look of uncertainty touches Mai's face. In the simple white dress hugging her gentle curves, her beauty is undeniable. She gestures to Caressa. "You remember my cousin, don't you?"

I should feel good that Mai's rushing to explain things to me, as if she cares what I think and how I'll react. Especially after the way we left things. But I can't see past the fact that once again, she's chosen her family over me or any other sensible option. Family that doesn't give a damn about her and only wants to use her. Granted, I don't know a thing about the cousin.

"Yes, I remember your cousin." I offer a hand to Caressa, and she grasps it firmly. Hers is a politician's too-warm handshake, as if she plans for us to be the best of friends once she's gotten every single penny out of my pocket.

"A pleasure," Caressa says. "I wouldn't have suggested coming here with Mai if I knew you were coming."

"And now what do we do?" Because I'm not going anywhere.

"Already taken care of, Ms. Bentley," Julie says, reminding me that she's still here and witnessing our little drama.

Before she finishes speaking, a man dressed in black and wearing the restaurant's signature gold name tag appears with a chair in his hands. With Mai and Caressa's cooperation, he pushes the table closer to the wall, adds the extra chair, and rearranges the place settings to make room for me. When he steps back, another uniformed person, a woman this time, is there with another place setting. The whole thing happens in a matter of seconds.

"Thank you, Julie." The new chair puts my back to the room, but I don't have it in me to complain.

"Of course, Ms. Bentley. We are here to ensure your comfort and dining pleasure."

"So far you're doing an excellent job."

"Perfect." A sincere yet professional smile warms her face. "Is there anything else I can get for you?"

I take my seat. "No, this is more than enough."

"Perfect," Julie says again. "Your waiter, Byron, will be here in a few minutes to take care of you." Then, with another smile, she drifts away.

All that and I didn't even have to threaten anyone. If this is anything to go by, Julie just might own the place in a few years. Or months.

Mai straightens the napkin in her lap and clears her throat. "You never responded to my last text," she says after a quick look at Caressa.

The cousin is doing a decent impression of not listening, sipping her wine then taking a piece of warm bread from the basket to butter on her plate. I can practically see her antenna go up, though.

But I don't have anything to hide as far as my relationship with Mai goes. Caressa can listen all she wants.

"I meant to respond but then got caught up doing some work for my tias." Before I left, they acted like they were never going to see me again in that house. "They'd love to have you come and spend some time with them, by the way. Tia Carmen said to let you know she'll make that sauce you like."

A smile blooms on Mai's face. Like my aunts, she loves family and thinks it's one of the most important relationships a person can have. It's a shame hers is trash.

"You were with your aunts in Mexico, right?" Caressa speaks up, and though I'm prepared to be very polite to her for Mai's sake, I wonder how the hell she knows where I've been.

"Yes, I was." Smoothing my napkin over my lap, I try to look politely at nosey Caressa.

"While I was visiting Abi at the family house, Caressa happened to drop by, and I ended up telling them both about..." Her lashes flutter down, and she looks at me from the corners of her eyes. "About how we're still finding the best way for us to fit together."

Caressa nods and tears into her lightly buttered bread. "Yes, then I asked her about your very interesting name."

Ah. "And that made you two talk about me visiting Mexico?"

Normally, I'm a bit more subtle about my suspicions. But this whole situation is turning me into an amateur. Then again, it's not every day I arrive at a date and find that I've been replaced. Mai and Caressa were carrying on just fine without me.

It doesn't take much for me to remember that they're distant cousins. Very distant.

On my left and close enough to touch, Mai butters a piece of bread, then abandons it on her plate instead of eating it.

Caressa tops up her glass of wine. "Did Mai tell you I'm learning Spanish?" She doesn't wait for me to answer. "I'm absolutely in love with the language, so when she told me you're from Mexico and what your name meant, I just threw a bunch of questions. In hindsight might have been a touch invasive. Sorry about that."

She doesn't look sorry, though. Her smile is warm and engaging, like she wants this situation to be some intimate joke we can laugh about years down the road once we've become the best of friends.

I don't trust her.

"Invasiveness seems like a Redstone family trait," I say with a smile that's a long way from being genuine.

But Caressa doesn't seem to care. "I know, right? The Redstones can be very...curious." That's one way of putting it. "Pretty soon, if they don't already, they'll know your favorite color and what side of the bed you like to sleep on."

"Blood red and right in the middle." I show her more of my teeth.

"Stop teasing her, Xóchitl." Mai flicks a piece of bread at me, and her cousin stares like Mai just grew a second head right here in front of the humans. Has Mai learned to shield herself from Caressa, too?

Our waiter shows up just then. After pouring my wine, he takes my order for each of the three courses and disappears again in a cloud of efficiency.

"This place is amazing," Mai says, smiling in the direction the waiter glided off to. "Despite the misunderstanding, I'm glad you're here to share it with me. It...it hasn't been the same without you here, even though Caressa has been great company."

Great company? I doubt that.

The cousin is pretty and charming. A Meta with enough power to make her seem interesting to a human. To Mai, she should just be a placeholder, and a disloyal one at that. I glance at the senator and wonder again at the strength of her mental abilities.

Was it a mental suggestion from her to Mai that changed the dinner reservations to half an hour earlier?

"Our little *misunderstanding* isn't reason enough for me to abandon you, Mai. Nothing is." I latch onto her gaze with mine. "Tia Ana told me to double check with you to make sure our date was still on, but I didn't think I needed to. We've never had to confirm with each other once we make plans. Once we decide to do something together, that's it."

"That's true," Mai says softly. Her fingers resting on the table twitch toward me then pull back to close in a loose fist.

Caressa clears her throat. "Um...I feel like I'm a bit of a third wheel here—"

"No, no. You're fine." Mai sits perfectly still with her back straight and her arms bracketing the small plate with her piece of buttered bread. She's comfortable with Caressa, but the woman doesn't have enough of her trust to see her completely relax. Bread-throwing incident aside. "Xóchitl and I have some unfinished business but please, don't let us run you off."

No, please do let us run you off.

But I have enough manners these days not to say the words out loud. The wine turns out to be a nice Crianza, fruity and flavorful. I take another sip and ignore Mai's silent plea for me to reassure Caressa she can stay. Catering to a near stranger's delicate feelings isn't something I'm up for right now.

I want to take Mai home so we can once and for all tear apart the thing separating us.

"All right, you convinced me to stay," Caressa says with a pleased smile. *Can this woman not read a room?* "I've wanted to check out this place forever, so I'm glad to just now get the chance."

Christ.

I give her a tight smile. When our waiter comes back, I order a double shot of tequila and tell him to leave the bottle on the table. Although it's nearly impossible for me to get drunk, I'm going to give it a really good try.

CHAPTER 17

CARESSA SEEMS TO ENJOY HER whole life at Pleasure and the Palate with me and Mai. I can't say the same, but that doesn't seem to matter to the cousin in the least.

At the end of what feels like the longest meal on earth, Caressa promises to take Mai and Abi to some converted mansion and museum to which she has VIP access. She and Mai have plans to talk the next morning and arrange the trip.

"Is she your best friend all of a sudden?" I ask, grumpy as hell and unwilling to hide it once we are finally alone in the foyer of Mai's apartment after Caressa dropped us off.

"She's family," Mai says, as we walk toward the elevator together. "Just about the only one, aside from Abi, who I can stand at the moment." She gives me a dry look.

I don't say a word. Her tolerance for idiocy is much higher than mine.

"I feel like she wasn't around much until very recently. What's going on?"

Mai shrugs and presses the button to summon the elevator. "Maybe she feels like I need a friend after you and I had our little disagreement the other day."

She would be better off kissing an asp than inviting another Redstone to be her friend.

My shoulders feel tight. Unhappiness sits like a stone in my belly, upsetting the meal I just had. "I wish you'd just call it a fight and stop using that strange euphemism. Disagreement. You make it sound like I'm into chicken while you only eat fish."

"True. I should be more specific. You having no qualms about killing people is definitely more serious than my possible preference for seafood over chicken."

"Is this really the approach you're going to take?"

"I can't think of any other way to bring it up. Besides, at least it gets you to stop talking about Caressa. Not everyone in my family has ulterior motives, you know."

"Don't worry, I have a mental pin stuck in your new best friend."

"At least it's not a knife," she mutters.

Damn, this conversation went left fast. What happened to the common ground we found in the restaurant?

The elevator chimes, and the doors slide open. Uncomfortable silence twists between us during the ride up to Mai's apartment. Once there, she unlocks the door and walks in, leaving me to trail after her.

Without turning on any lights, she kicks off her high heels with a clatter against the wooden floors and leans back against the side of the couch. Moonlight pours in through the window to limn her body in silver. Her bare toes, tipped in red, invite intimacy, memories of having her feet in my lap and the sound of laughter in my ear. I cross my arms and lean back against the front door to stop myself from coming close.

"I missed you," she says finally.

The words unfurl a quiet relief in my chest. "I missed you, too."

"But I still disagree with how you handled things at the school." Whatever softness or good feelings from the restaurant have apparently worn off.

"We're lovers." My fingers dig into my arms. "We don't have to agree on everything. Just who gets to tie who up and then take out the recycling."

"Don't be dismissive, please."

"I'm not being dismissive, I'm being myself." Hasn't she always said she likes that I'm always *me* with her? "The things that happened at the school don't mean very much to me. In my job, I have to make split-second decisions all the time, and those decisions leave no room to let a proven killer go free."

"So you just kill them."

"You know that's exactly what enforcers do, Mai. Don't pretend to be naïve."

"God!" She pushes herself off the couch and stalks away, bare feet slapping against the hardwood. Any softness about her is gone.

I track her agitated movements, not shifting from my place in front of the door. Subconsciously trying to keep her in the apartment with me? Who knows? That's why it's called subconscious.

Mai paces back toward me, then away. "You may be investigator and executioner in the Meta community but you're not that here, Xóchitl. Here, you're a college professor." Her eyes snap in the moonlight. "Leave the humans to the humans. You had no right killing that boy."

"So, I should've let him kill you?"

She's crazier than her mother if she thinks I'd let anyone, let alone a human, get close enough to hurt her. I regret absolutely nothing that happened that day. Certainly not the boy I flung through a glass window and splatted like a bad meal on the pavement twenty stories below.

"He couldn't hurt me! None of his bullets came anywhere close. You know that." She tries to stare me down. "Now which of us is being deliberately naïve?"

"I'm being naïve knowing you're not as indestructible as you think?"

Mai is like a newborn let loose in the world of rampaging monsters and indifferent gods. She thinks she knows exactly what's going on and how to protect herself, but she has no idea.

"I've changed," she growls at me. "I'm much better than I was. I'm not the same Mai you were able to sneak up on and push around."

It's damn near an invitation to prove her wrong. Without trying, I can think of five ways to get her on her back or dead. The breath abruptly stutters in my chest. The thought of her broken or lifeless…

"That may be true," I say when I can speak again. "But what you do now as Mercy, taking risks you never took before, is foolish enough."

She draws in a hissing breath. "This isn't about me being Mercy. It's about you having enough compassion not to kill and having enough mercy in your own heart to save humans from being killed when you're able to."

And now we get to the real reason for her anger.

It's not about the boy or my lack of compassion or anything else she's said tonight.

It's what I didn't do for the other humans and for the girl who died in her arms that's upset her the most.

Now it's my turn to pace back and forth. My high heels ring against her pretty wooden floor, gouging the pale wood with each step. Why is she being so frustrating?

"I can't save everyone. That's not my job, and I'm not going to pretend that it is just to get you to like me better."

She grabs my arm to stop my pacing and steps even more into my space. "This is not about me liking you better and you know that. It doesn't make sense for you not to save people when you can."

Her fingers dig into my elbow, but I allow the unfamiliar pain instead of pulling away. "Just because you're able to do something doesn't mean you should," I say.

"That's *exactly* what it fucking means," Mai growls. "Why don't you understand that?" She makes another sound of frustration and her voice rises. "I hate it's so easy for you to kill, Xóchitl. Especially when you took your revenge as the Absolution Killer. It's subhuman."

*Sub*human? Is this what she thinks of me?

Slowly, I release a calming breath. "Actually, the desire to kill is one of the most human impulses." A second breath expands my lungs, but it doesn't help the dangerous combination of anger and hurt rising in me. "You know, I think we're done here for the night."

"No!" Mai rushes toward me, and I slip quickly sideways and away from the door until the open window is to my back instead.

"I didn't mean…" But she can't finish the sentence because she did mean every word.

"It's fine. We'll talk more another time." And then, because it hurts too much to do otherwise, I leave, leaping high up to the open window and out into the cold evening.

CHAPTER 18

My anger doesn't take me very far. Only to the rooftop of Mai's apartment building, staring down into the quiet darkness and wishing for things that could not be.

Subhuman. That's what she thinks of me and still lets me touch her?

The cocktail of emotions writhes dangerously in my stomach, and it's all I can do not to lean my head over the side of the roof and heave up my dinner. But no. I have more control than that. Or I used to before I met Mai.

A sound coming from the window I'd just slipped through jerks my attention downward. It's Mai. No, Mercy.

My woman's alter ego sits poised on the edge of the open window. From above, I see the sloping line of her back, her head bent as she seems to listen to the sounds of the city. In her oxblood skin, she's costumed and on the hunt for some lost lambs to rescue and distract her from the tension between us. Because I'm a fool, I follow her.

It's a quiet night in Atlanta, though, and all Mai is able to find is a coldly calculating man threatening his wife with a pistol he doesn't even bother to take from the gun safe.

Radiating tension and discontent, Mai perches on the porch of a Grant Park bungalow and watches what's going on in the house while I watch her.

A man is lecturing his wife. "Don't go out with your friends again without my permission. You will respect me and my time. I gave you this nice house and that ice on your finger, and I can easily take it all away with one bullet."

The man sits in his armchair with the television on a cooking show. Oil splashes in the pan on-screen while his wife sits in a green velvet armchair, designed to look like a throne, with her hands crossed over a knee and her eyes fixed on her husband.

Her eyes are cold, but even from far away I can see the bone-deep fear in them. Looks like she's been putting up with him for a long time.

The man waves a hand without taking his eyes off the television. A king dismissing his subject. "Now, go and put on the outfit I left for you on the bed. Make the recipe on page fourteen of this week's cookbook, and don't get the dress dirty. Be the good little wife I pay you to be."

It's all terrifying in an everyday sort of way. The man is handsome. The woman beautiful. Their house is perfect.

When the frightened woman disappears into a far bedroom, Mai calls the police, says she's a concerned neighbor, then slips away from the house and practically flies through trees and across rooftops to get back to her apartment.

Despite my roiling stomach that refuses to settle down, I follow her every step.

CHAPTER 19

Despite my decision to stay away from Mai, I keep circling back to her, and by default, to the Redstones.

Before our fight, she asked me to come to another one of her family events. Because I'm an idiot, I said yes without hesitation. After that ridiculous dinner a few weeks ago, how much worse could things get?

The heels of my ankle boots clatter up the stone walkway. Flower-scented air brushes my face, and I inhale the sweetness with every step, my heart tripping over itself in anticipation of being in the same space with Mai again.

The park is wide and lush: a pretty space with flowers bright and blooming everywhere, butterflies kissing wide-open petals, and the low sound of classic jazz from over hedge. It's beautiful, and I feel as if I don't belong.

"Good afternoon." A pleasant enough Meta host greets me at the entrance to the garden, an archway with sweet-smelling roses dripping down, their thorns hidden or cut off.

"I'm here for the Redstone event. Xóchitl Bentley."

"Of course." He doesn't bother to consult any sort of list that I can see, only bows to me with another smile and invites me past.

As promised by the high arbor and red, red roses, the setting of the garden party is almost too beautiful. Flowers everywhere. At least two dozen people in spring colors. A long table set up away from the sun with every kind of food imaginable.

The air throbs and hums from the presence of so many power-rich Metas in one place.

Jazz plays from speakers that reach every part of the private garden. Small tables set for four and covered by deep purple tablecloths rest under wide, white umbrellas. The conversations around me happen in hushed, polite tones. Everyone is dressed in rich-casual.

Where is Mai?

My mind automatically reaches out for her. And encounters a brick wall. I stand still, floundering in the proof of how much she's pushed me away.

Swallowing the thick pain, I use my eyes to find her. And there she is.

Pretty in a yellow dress and bright red heels, she's talking with her sister. Abi, animated as ever, describes something while her hands wave around her head and her teeth flash in a long laugh. Her tie-dyed cotton dress is a loud splash in the sea of mostly white.

I head toward them.

"You did manage to make it after all." Mai's brother pops out of the greenery near me. If he was hoping to scare me, he's missed it by a mile.

"Cayman." I can't even add the usual "nice to see you" because it's definitely not.

At one point, I'd had vague hopes similar to Mai's for her brother to be less of an asshole. Being unknowingly complicit in Ethan's attempted assassination of Mai seemed to be something of a nasty surprise to Cayman. At the time, it looked like he took stock of things, especially the way he'd been treating Mai for years. But then something happened. Mai doesn't know what, and I don't, either. I'm sure I could find out, but for what purpose? Nothing would change.

"I didn't think you'd come," Cayman says to me with a grin. "At least Mai didn't mention it. I expected you guys to show up at these kinds of things together."

"I'm sure your expectations are rarely my reality," I say with a shrug.

His smile slips a notch. Then it widens, warning me he's about to say something I won't like.

"I know you were a little upset that we asked Mai to step in and speak on Ethan's behalf at the hearing—"

"Upset?" What a conveniently tame word. "You could say that. Weren't you there to see how Ethan tried to tear Mai's head off? Didn't that convince you he was even a little guilty of what the enforcers accused him of?"

"He's a Redstone. With us, things usually aren't what they seem." He made a face as if tasting something bad just before spitting it out. "Besides, the family doesn't always have the luxury to do what's right."

If that's not a commentary on what's wrong with this world and this family, I don't know what is.

"I doubt I'm telling you anything new, but as Head Family of the region, you should do what's right for the Metas here," I say. "How long can the other Families look to the Redstones for leadership when you allow a killer to go free just because he's a member of a powerful family? Your family."

Cayman winces but doesn't back down. "Do you know how rare it is to have someone as powerful as Ethan now? We're dying out as a power-rich people."

Is that all this is about? Sacrificing Mai for the sake of a few parlor tricks?

"And so what? Harvest the boy's spunk if that's something you're so worried about. Don't spare him so he can kill again."

Cayman's eyes narrow as he gives me a considering look. "You're not all that you seem, are you?"

"I'm angry if that's what you're asking."

He lets out a huff of laughter. "And here I thought you were just another boring, barely Meta who Mai decided to mess around with in her endless search for mediocrity."

Heat pulses in my clenched fist. "You really are an asshole, aren't you?"

His eyes bug out a little bit. Like he isn't used to people telling him the truth. "You're definitely not what I thought when we first met."

"Hm. I was being nice for Mai."

His look is pure speculation. "I guess you stopped being nice."

"Not yet, but close."

The sound of Mai's laughter suddenly rises up and claims my attention. Cayman fades to the back of my awareness and all I feel is Mai. Not in my mind like I want her, but that flush of goosebumps over my skin and woman's scent of her on the air.

Time to break this stupid stalemate.

"Well, it was almost fun chatting with you, Cayman. I'm sure we'll do it again soon." Then I leave him to find the reason I'm swimming with these sharks.

"Xóchitl!" Abi waves to get my attention before I get too far. She walks toward me like a woman on a mission, her long hippie dress kicking out with each step.

I meet her halfway. "Nice weather for a family fun day."

Her eyes flash with faint humor. "I don't even know what this is supposed to be. We have these informal get-togethers here at least once a month so we can see each other and help build strength and unity as a family, but I don't see it doing any good."

"As far as I can tell, except for Mai, the Redstones are plenty united." Their strength is a given.

Regret flashes in her eyes before she slides them away from mine. "It's not—it's not what you think. My brother is jealous, and it's turning him into an ass."

What's Mandaia's excuse? The question crouches behind my teeth, but I push it back to play nice. "What does he have to be jealous about?" I ask instead. "He suddenly has a burning desire for his mother's apathy, too, or something?"

So, playing nice doesn't always work out so well for me.

"It's *so* the opposite," Abi says, apparently not catching my venom. "In the last couple of months, Mom hasn't stopped talking about Mai. You know, about all the new stuff she can do and saying how much she regrets not being there for Mai when Mai needed her most—whatever *that* means."

A shrug hitches her shoulder and a look of bewilderment turns down the corners of her mouth. "She says this stuff to me and Cayman, but never to Mai." Her eyes dart to where her brother is chatting with someone whose face I can't see. He looks aggressively cheerful, reaching over to slap the man's shoulder while drinking from his manly glass of dark liquor. "Cayman hates it. He's used to having all our parents' attention."

"Maybe he just needs a good punch in the face to teach him that sharing is caring. Or at least good for his health."

Whatever she catches in my tone brings her chin up. "It's not just Cayman, is it? You don't like any of us very much."

"No, I don't." Then because she's not my enemy and Mai loves her, I add, "Can you blame me?"

She pauses, chewing on her bottom lip like she's actually thinking about it. "I guess I can't. It…it's still so strange to see what my family has become while I've been away. Dad seems so emotionally absent from everything while Mom is harder and colder than I've ever seen. Most days, my brother is a raging dick to everyone around him." Her lashes flutter down to hide her eyes and she shrugs, conveying a sad hopelessness that makes me almost want to hug her in reassurance. "I dunno, maybe we've always been like this and I never noticed."

I cross my arms to keep the hug to myself. "It's not for me to say. All I know is that I want Mai safe and happy, and that's hard to have with her family around." My head tilts in her direction. "You being the obvious exception."

"But how fucked up is that, though? Why can't we just be normal?"

"My aunt would say normal is boring."

A tremor of a smile touches her mouth. "But at least it's safe."

I can't argue with her there.

She stops trying to chew her own lip off and puts on a look of determined cheerfulness. "Come on, I'll take you over to Mai."

Abi doesn't try to touch me, but she steps closer as we head over to where Mai stands off by herself, checking something on her phone.

"You know, sometimes I just want to run back to Switzerland and leave all this strange drama behind," Abi says.

"Why don't you?"

Abi shoves her hands in the pockets of her dress. "It's stupid, but I don't want to leave Mai alone again."

"That's not stupid. It's love. I know she'd be sad if you left."

Hanging out with her sister these past few months has been good for Mai. She laughs more. It shows her what family is supposed to feel like. These outings with Abi have given her some of the greatest moments of happiness in the months we've been together.

Other than when she's with me, obviously.

When we reach Mai, she's just putting away her phone. All around her, the other Redstones and hangers-on drift like sharks waiting for blood to hit the water.

"Look who I found," Abi announces with a smile when Mai looks up with a kind of twisted hope on her face. At least that's what I think it is.

"Hi." I drift close to her, close enough to let her know that I'm here, and unless she throws me to wolves, I'll always be here. "Sorry I'm late." I offer her myself, soft-eyed and open, hoping she didn't tell them I wasn't coming at all.

"It's okay," Mai says. "I wasn't sure about..." Her words taper off with a shrug, and all I want to do is hold her and tell her that with me she never has to be uncertain about anything. But it's a fantasy that doesn't even work out in my own mind.

"You're right on time, I think." This time it's Caressa who joins our party.

Abi waves at her cousin with a cheek-plumping smile. "I didn't think you'd come today, Caressa. Didn't you say you had to be in DC this week for work?"

"I did, but just shuffled around some things in my schedule. Didn't want to miss the annual garden party."

"Really?" Mai slides her cousin a questioning look. "You hate these things. Something about the bugs and too-hot sun."

Caressa makes a dismissive motion of her shoulders bared in a jade, strapless jumpsuit. "A girl can change her mind."

"I guess…" Mai looks doubtful.

Caressa's eyes narrow for a moment before her face smooths itself into its usual pleasant blandness. "Xóchitl, I heard about the gun incident at your university the other day. You must have been scared witless."

A minute flinch moves through Mai's body, something that would have gone unnoticed unless you were paying attention. I'm paying attention.

I send a wave of calm to Mai before I remember she's locked me out. "It *was* bad but the school is doing everything it can so that kind of thing won't happen again." Silently, I will Caressa to leave it alone.

But apparently, I sent my *shut the hell up* thoughts to the wrong person.

"I heard about it, too. News about it was on all the TV stations," Abi says with a sympathetic sound. "Those poor kids!"

Caressa nods, her forehead wrinkled in concern. "In the end, the boy shooter was killed, and dozens of students were saved. It would've been much worse if some brave souls hadn't stepped forward to help."

"From what I saw on the news, it was a crazy nightmare. Something we never thought would happen so close to us." Abi puts her arm around Mai's waist and pulls her close. "The usual batch of meaningless words were flying around afterward, along with a complete *lack* of discussion on gun reform."

"Business as usual," I say with a pointed look at Caressa. "Isn't that part of your job, Senator? To see that it's more than words that end up on the front page then forgotten once the blood on the pavement is dry?"

"When you put it that way…" Caressa's tone is amused, and she turns her eyes on me, just enough to feel a vague pull that lets me know she's trying to influence me. *Amateur hour.* "I'm doing what I can," she says, and the mental pull on me intensifies.

"Try harder."

"Xóchitl!" From the circle of her sister's embrace, Mai gasps with a tap on my hand that feels like a kiss. It's been forever since we touched. "Stop being rude."

I touch the spot where she tapped me, curling my fingers over the skin to try and prolong the sensation. Her eyes dip down to watch the movement, and I feel her soften just the tiniest bit.

"I'm only being myself, love," I tell her softly. "Isn't that what we agreed the last time we had this discussion?"

Mai opens her mouth to comment, but Caressa cuts her off.

"Well, it's not like Xóchitl is that nice a person," her cousin says, buttery smooth and cool.

This is a warning. And I should pay more attention. There's a hint of something from Caressa that makes my neck prickle. But Mai is here and angry. I can barely focus on the world as it is when we're fighting like this. Especially when all I want is to pull her into my arms and out of this garden of snakes, tell her that none of this other stuff matters. Just us.

But she wouldn't agree to leave with me and so I'd be left alone, stuck on the outside of her world with my splintered piece of our love.

"What did you say?" Mai's mildly reproving look abruptly shifts from me to Caressa.

"You know it's true, Mai," Caressa says with a click of her tongue and then a smile to make it all seem like a joke. "This is a dangerous person you brought into our lives. All this time the enforcers have been telling us that Ethan was the Absolution Killer, but we've had the real killer here all along." The edges of her normally flirtatious smile are sharp.

Panic flares in Mai's eyes, then fury. At the same time, Abi gasps and takes a jerking step away from me.

"I don't know what you're talking about, Caressa." A hint of betrayal burns the edges of Mai's words.

"It's okay, Mai." The new sharpness to Caressa's smile could cut glass. "You don't have to lie for her. It's not something you're good at anyway."

What the hell?

"Is this true, Mai?" Abi confronts her sister in a whirl of brightly colored cotton. Her wide eyes flit between me and Mai.

"We have a monster in our midst." Caressa jumps in before Mai can speak. Her voice is loud like she's shouting to the entire city of Atlanta. Making sure that the whole clan of power-rich Redstones is able to hear the damaging truth she's dropped like an atomic bomb in the place where it would do the most damage.

Mandaia Redstone is suddenly at Caressa's side, looking spring-appropriate in a pale pink dress. "What's happening here?"

Everyone else in the little arbor is paying attention. Subtly, they begin to creep closer to us. Well, maybe not so subtly.

"This is who killed Uncle Stephen, not Ethan." Caressa gestures to me with a languid wave of her hand.

Already narrowing with suspicion, Mandaia's amber eyes go flat and hard. After a scouring look at me then Mai, she turns to Caressa. "Do you know this for sure?"

My mind skitters to the last time I saw Caressa. She was all smiles and helpfulness when she dropped me and Mai off at the condo.

What happened between then and now?

How does she know about the Absolution Killer?

She doesn't seem the smartest one in the bunch, and I've been careful not to let Absolution out of the box since Ethan was arrested for her kills.

"I'm very sure." A tiny smile curls up the corners of Caressa's lips. She looks smug. "Xóchitl and Mai were talking about it, and I recorded everything. I can play it for you if you like."

She heard us talking? Where? Then the evening I last saw Caressa rushes back to me. Every word Mai and I spoke to each other in what I thought was the privacy of her damn living room.

When this is over, Caressa is *dead*.

Mai's face is a careful blank, but I can see the subtle tension at the corners of her mouth.

Taking careful steps away from me and Mai, Caressa keeps talking. "I actually have the tape right here. We might as well have a listen." She reaches into her delicate little purse and pulls out her phone. The conversation is evidently all cued up to go because all she does is tap the phone's screen a couple of times before Mai's recorded voice spills out.

"*I hate it's so easy for you to kill, Xóchitl. Especially when you took your revenge as the Absolution Killer. It's subhuman.*"

A tap of Caressa's finger cuts off the audio. "There you have it," she says. "My undeniable proof."

A rattling of anger rises up from different corners of the arbor, but even with the rage twisting her face after listening to her own daughter confirm Caressa's accusation, Mandaia ignores it.

"How and why did you get this information, Caressa?" she rasps.

Suddenly, Caressa doesn't look so certain. "I-I've been working with Ethan to...to help clear his name," she stammers but quickly gains control over herself. "I know he isn't the Absolution Killer and I want everyone else to know, too."

"Go on," Mandaia says with a motion of her chin. Waves of fire rise and fall in her eyes.

"I've had somebody following Mai at the school where she works. At first, I-I thought it was fitting punishment to get her fired. With rumors and that kind of thing." At Mai's hiss and the audible pop of her clenched fists, Caressa backs away. "You can't have the life you want when Ethan is facing execution, Mai." Caressa shakes her head, thick and shining hair slithering over her shoulders. "The world isn't fair, I know that. But it makes me *sick* to see you in love and happy while Ethan stands to lose his life." With each word that drips from her lips, Caressa becomes more and more calm. "I wanted that school to fire you and ruin everything you have in the human world." Caressa slips her phone back into her purse and turns back to Mandaia, a look of utter confidence on her face. "She deserves to be ruined after she helped to pin the murders her lover committed on my Ethan."

My Ethan, huh?

"I didn't hear your voice on that recording," Mandaia says to me, her own calm absolute but a sign of a rage more powerful than anything Caressa could ever express. "Is any of this true?"

"All of this is true," Caressa insists. "You heard her say it."

Mandaia and I both ignore her.

"Only a few months ago, Ethan tried to kill Mai. I'm sure you and your little boy"—I tilt my head toward a glowering Cayman—"saw that much."

"That doesn't answer my question."

"Well, that's the only answer you're getting out of me." Evenly balancing my weight on the balls of my feet, I prepare for the physical confrontation that's as inevitable as my next breath.

Mandaia slips off her pretty pink jacket and drops it on the ground behind her. "Believe me, I can get more out of you, Xóchitl." She sneers my name. Power crackles around her like static electricity, and, although nothing about her changes physically, she suddenly seems two feet taller. "When I'm done with you, you'll be pouring out all of your secrets and begging me to stop the pain."

Pain? A laugh bubbles out of my throat, bitter and unamused. What kind of pain could she inflict that having my parents then my sister ripped out of my life haven't already brought?

My inner fire rushes through me, and a haze of heat distorts Mandaia's image in front of my eyes. Then everything gets clearer, becomes as sharp as a knife edge about to taste blood. If they think I'll be easy prey, then they have no idea who they're dealing with.

A powerful wind surges up around Mandaia, and the grass begins to frantically grow around my feet, twisting to grab at my ankles. Shit! I leap back and bump into an immovable body. Cayman. Then he yelps at the same moment the smell of singed flesh and burnt grass rises in the air. Bet he won't touch me again before thinking twice.

From the corner of my eye, I see a swarm of thick, thorny vines heavy with red roses fly toward me. Then freeze barely an inch from Mai's face.

She stands in front of me, her arms spread wide, her hands replaced by long, wicked-looking blades.

"I'm sorry, Mother." With the hem of her yellow dress whipping frantically in her mother's breeze, she matches Mandaia, calm for calm. Both their gazes spark like the blazing red center of a forge. "But you'll have to go through me first."

Shock nearly drops me where I stand.

CHAPTER 20

THIS ISN'T MAI'S FIGHT. I can't let her pretend that it is, no matter how much I want to.

"Step aside, love." Despite the blood thundering in my ears, the urge to crush her to me in gratitude, I gently push her away. Or at least I try to, but she doesn't move.

I'm not going anywhere. Her words unfurl in my mind. A fist squeezes my heart tight and a syrupy gladness trickles through me. She's let me back into her mind. I try not to grin like a fool, but from the murderous look on her mother's face, I've failed miserably.

The vines thick with vicious thorns twist and thrash in the air just in front of Mai's face, snakes hungry for a kill.

"Yes, Mai. Step aside and let me deal with this murderer. She is nothing to betray your family over." The air quivers around Mandaia. Her clawed fingers tense at her sides as if she's ready to rip the world apart to get to me.

"I won't let you hurt her," Mai growls.

The wolves are circling. Redstones creeping closer with every flash of Mandaia's eyes. All it takes is for her to give the signal and they'll be on top of me. But that also means they'll be on top of Mai. A coldness grips my belly at the thought. She can't become a casualty of this war I have with her family.

A few quick footsteps pull me from the protection of Mai's body. The thorns thrash through the air toward me.

"No!" Lightning quick, Mai slashes away the barbed thigh-sized vines before they can connect. Harmless pieces of green, wet with sap, drop to the grass. "Mother, stop!"

Her mother only growls and presses forward. At least with her body. Her vines twist and growl restlessly in the air above her, the sound of the thick trunks rubbing together like the hissing of snakes.

My chest shudders with the frantic pounding of my heart. "Mandaia, you caused this," I shout. I watch the thick vines twitching far too close to Mai. "Ethan Redstone is a spoiled monster. Stephen Redstone was a beast who preyed on his own kind. When you tried to drag Mai into the hearing to testify for Ethan, you only proved that you're a monster just like them."

"It's not like that!" Abi's voice rises suddenly above the cacophonous sound of the vines. "My family is being pressured to free Ethan. They don't want to." Her voice drops off. "At least, I don't think they do."

"Don't tell them anything, Abi!" Cayman shouts from behind me.

"What?" But Mai jerks part of her attention to her sister, not completely taking her eyes off Mandaia. "Are you sure?"

"I…was going to tell you once you got here, but then you seemed so sad. I just didn't want to make you feel worse." She shrugs helplessly with the beginning of tears in her voice.

"Who exactly is *they*? What's going on?" Mai's hands are still bladed and deadly, but they drop away from the threat as she looks between Abi and their mother.

"Now's probably not the time, babe," I say. The Redstones circle closer to the soundtrack of the hissing thorny vines. "Your family is out for blood and I don't think they'll stop with mine."

"We don't hurt our own." Cayman's furious lie is as obvious as his ridiculous taste in clothes.

"Mai, let's just go."

"Do you think we'll let you leave just like that?" Cayman snarls. He's closer to Mai than he deserves to be, and my muscles twitch with the urge to kick his knee out.

"Mai." I touch the unyielding small of her back. "Leave with me. Now."

The vines hiss and twist and shake even more, the noise of their agitation rising and expanding in the arbor.

"You're not going anywhere." Mandaia gestures with a tilt of her head to the Redstones surrounding me, the enclosed garden, and the host at the gate smiling as if he has more important things to worry about than the bloodbath about to happen.

Mandaia's overconfidence is hilarious. They don't know their hold on me is like water in an outstretched hand.

"Mai?"

"I don't want them to hurt you, but I think they will."

Cayman and the others move restlessly, pushing closer, crushing the grass underfoot and stirring up the scent of green. It obviously pisses them off that we're ignoring them. The air crackles with tension. Any moment now, they're going to pounce and rip us apart.

"Mai, trust me now like you did before."

"I never stopped trusting you," she says.

"Good." One quick step forward and I'm pressed flat against her back. Then I teleport us out of the garden of snakes. The cool space of her apartment slowly appears around us. The sunlight. Her furniture. My Aztec blanket draped over the couch.

Once the cold of the shift has passed, Mai looks up at me with surprise swimming in her eyes. The blades below her elbows transform once again into arms. "I didn't know you could do that."

"I know."

"But…"

"Remember when Ethan appeared out of nowhere that afternoon, the first day you invited me back to your place for sex?"

Incredibly, despite the chaos and danger we just left behind, her cheeks darken with color. "Yes, how could I forget that?" Images from that afternoon unfurl in her mind like a beautiful ribbon. Our meeting in the street by arranged accident. My hand on hers while her cousin, Ethan, lurked around us. Then later, in her bed. Both of us breathless, clumsy with the uncertainty of new lovers.

"Only my hand on you prevented him from teleporting you off that street. As you know, sometimes like powers can cancel each other out in a confrontation."

Brow furrowed, she steps back from me. "I wish you'd trust me with things like this, Xóchitl."

"I do, Mai." How can she doubt how much I trust her when all I've done the past few months is show her just that? The backs of my fingers brush her cheek. "I trust you more than any lover who'd ever claimed to want me for more than the things I can do. I—"

The sudden throb of the space being disrupted cuts me off the same instant a horde of Redstones descends into the room. They flood from the kitchen, from the bedroom, through the window. From everywhere like rats.

"Mai!" I shout her name just as rough hands grip me. A howl tears from my throat, my skin heats, and whoever touched me screams along with me, but that only lasts a moment before something latches onto my neck. I shrug it off, moving too quickly for most to see.

Someone tears Mai from my arms and flings her across the room. A framed photo of Mai and her sister tumbles to the floor and shatters. Another Redstone grabs Mai's arms and feet and pin her to the wall.

"Don't let her get hurt!" Someone shouts. Probably her mother.

But it's too late for that. Even through the haze of fire in front of my eyes, I can see the pain and fury in Mai's gaze. Her mouth flies open, and her eyes squeeze shut. She screams my name again, and barbs erupt from her arms, her fingernails, sharp and dangerous, glinting silver and chrome in the light. Everything about her is sharp and painful.

The Redstones are everywhere.

I keep my body in motion, bouncing off the air like a ping pong ball, past their hands, trying to get away and hurt as many of them as possible at the same time. My entire body is a sizzling furnace. They touch me and they burn.

"Grab her!"

But they're making a mistake if they think I'm as easy as all that. Hands latch onto me. A woman screams as her fingers, suddenly super-heated from my skin, sizzle and fall off. Something sharp cuts down my side and burns a thousand times more than fire. The flavor of blood explodes in my mouth as I bite down on my tongue to keep the scream inside.

But I don't go down.

A somersault over the couch and I'm flinging myself across the room, knocking over a vase, the television. Glass shatters, and pieces dig into my skin. Already I'm healing, my skin pushing out the pieces of glass, getting rid of anything that doesn't belong.

"She's too fast."

"Slow her down, then!"

Cayman is suddenly there. Watching from a corner of the room. He doesn't touch me, but he doesn't have to. He could break my bones with just one look. My only hope is to move too fast for him to properly see me. I leap around the ruined room, slipping from hand to hand, dodging lances of ice and stinging barbs that fly through the room, burning everyone who touches me.

"Take her!" A breathless order. "Alive or dead, I don't care. Just make sure Mai isn't hurt."

That word again. Hurt.

It means so much more than they think it does. The Redstones think only they have the right to hurt Mai and that this pain, mostly emotional, isn't as real as being punched in the face or abandoned to a horrific childhood.

A scream rings out.

Mai! Where is she?

Stupid. I shouldn't have brought her here. That was stupid and predictable. But Cayman and the others followed us sooner than I planned.

"I'm going to gut you!" A pretty girl with bright lipstick suddenly appears in front of me, a chair raised over her head. She slams the wooden chair toward me, but I easily dodge it.

The place is chaos. Broken furniture and cracked walls. Blood in deep red splashes across the floors. The siren of Mai's screams rattles the apartment. Three people hold her pinned to the wall, all doing their best to avoid the blades sprouting and slashing all over her body.

I have to get her out of here. Damn her family.

Twisting in mid-air, still untouchable, I head toward her, my hands burning and ready to incinerate all three members of her loving family keeping her prisoner.

"Stop her!"

A cresting wave of growls rises up around me. The window near Mai slams shut.

"Knock her out! She can't escape if she's unconscious." As if I'd abandon Mai here with them.

"Easy for you to say. I can't even see her, she's moving so damn fast!"

Mai's eyes fly open, and her sudden and sharp fear burns through me like acid. There's someone new in the apartment. Someone dangerous. And they're close.

"Xóchitl, the window! Just go—!"

Then something hits me hard in the face. Pain starbursts behind my cheek, and I crash into…nothing, ricocheting into an immovable and invisible wall before landing flat on my back. Then I can't hear a thing. More than half a dozen Redstones surround me, crowding me. I'm trapped in a bubble of space, my body glowing, my powers useless.

On my hands and knees now, I take in as much air as I can, gasping. Around me, Cayman and a few unfamiliar Redstones creep closer. His ugly jacket is ripped in places, and he's lost one of his shoes. His relatives don't look much better.

Even though every part of me hurts, my lip curls in satisfaction.

"Let her go!" Mai twists like a wild thing against the three who have her pinned.

"Why would we let a criminal go when she's all but confessed?" Cayman shouts back.

"I haven't confessed to a damn thing and you know it," I growl between desperate breaths.

Damn. My head is swimming. My arms tremble and can barely hold me up.

"You should save your breath," Caressa says, calm as you please. She's managed to stay out of the fight and looks as fresh as a prom queen at her coronation. "Not that you'll be able to use it for much longer."

My lips curl back in a snarl, hungry to spill her blood. She shouldn't be here. Not in the place where Mai and I have made love, confessed secrets to each other, cooked and cared for each other.

Anger floods through me like lava. "Fuck you!"

Then my senses begin to dim. My vision goes dark at the edges. My quiet sips of breath become desperate gasps.

"Stop it!" Mai's shouts sound far away. "You're killing her!"

"That's the idea."

My shaking arms give out, and I drop to my belly with a heavy thud. The hardwood floor slams up into my face, and my sweaty cheek slides across it. My breath hitches, body goes slack. The only sound is my desperate breathing while I feel the Redstones creeping closer. Their feet. Their deep breaths. Their powers at the ready to finish me off.

"Mai…" Her name fumbles off my tongue.

She screams again. At least I think so, but I can barely hear it.

My heart slows. My breath. My breath…stops.

Seconds tick by.

"I think she's done."

"No!" Mai's shout penetrates the fog blanketing my senses.

I'm still here, baby. Don't worry. At least that's what I want to say. But I can't move. I can't speak. My breath is gone. My eyes are shut.

More seconds.

"Let's just be sure." Footsteps creep closer. Hard fingers jerk in my hair and yank my head back. Hot breath huffs against my face as whoever it is peers close to check for signs of life. There has to be pain, but I can't feel any of it.

"We don't have time for that. The cops will be here soon."

"Kendra dampened the noise. None of the humans heard a thing."

"We should torture her, make her confess to what Caressa said she did."

"She's not going to talk. That much is pretty damn obvious." Cayman this time.

"And what about the enforcers?"

"What about them? Do you want to just turn her into them like this, dead or as close as?"

"That's not what I'm talking about. They'll hear about this soon and come for us. We can't kill a Meta and expect it to go unchallenged."

"They'll know we had no choice. Especially when they find out the wrong person is in jail for Absolution's crimes."

"We can deal with all that later. For now, let's get rid of this."

They're talking about me. But I can't do a thing about it. I'm trapped in my body. Can't move. Mai is screaming, and I hear the slam and thud of flesh on flesh as she struggles to get away. She's screaming my name.

"What if the humans find her?" someone asks.

Mandaia Redstone is ice. "That's not our problem."

Rough hands handle me, then air rushes over my face, my body. I'm flying into space, out the window.

Falling. Like the boy who came to the school with his gun.

Like trash. Spilling out of Mai's home, out of her life.

The day is bright, incandescent afternoon light that burns through my closed lids, and it feels like I'm flying into the sun. Then falling away from it. The ground rushes up.

An agony of flesh meeting pavement.

Then nothing.

CHAPTER 21

SOMETHING IS MISSING. A PIECE of me I didn't even know existed. And now it's gone.

God, it hurts. This phantom limb.

Darkness swims all around me, slipping between me and the missing piece that's just out of reach. My mouth opens to call for it by name, yawning in desperation, but the darkness slips inside, choking me. I can't even scream.

CHAPTER 22

"I KNEW THAT GIRL WOULD get you into trouble." A familiar voice pulls me slowly out of the darkness.

"Tia Ana?" My throat feels raw. Speaking hurts. Actually, everything hurts.

"Who else, my flower?" A hand touches my brow, and I flinch from the pain. My tia hisses an apology. "Rest now. We're taking you somewhere safe."

We?

Gradually, I notice the sensation of movement. A rocking, like I'm in some kind of vehicle but I can't see anything. Black-out windows?

I take a deep breath. Bad idea. Nausea rushes up, but I clench my mouth shut and breathe until the urge to vomit goes away.

My body is one massive ache. My limbs feel rubbery and useless, and the part of my brain that controls my powers feels scooped out. Empty. Even my teeth hurt.

"Where am I?"

"Someplace safe for now." My tia hovers above me in white. Her hair is a silver spill over one shoulder, and her eyes look like stars.

"Am I broken?" My voice is like a child's. The aches in my body make me feel like crawling back into the womb, and not in a sexy way.

"A little." She ghosts her fingers over my cheek but doesn't touch me. I'm so grateful for that I almost cry. "But nothing we can't fix. Rest now. When you wake up, things should be better."

"Okay." The echo of my own voice makes my head hurt.

The pillow cradles my head when I sag into it, and sleep quickly reaches up to pull me back under.

When I wake again, it's dark. Real dark this time, not just the dark that comes from having your brains rattled around in your head like pop in a bottle. My lips are dry. The ache in my head has eased to a rumbling train instead of a death metal concert.

The room is mostly bare, and small, with a darkened lamp on the bedside table, hardwood floors, and walls the color of coffee with too much cream. A single window sits opposite the full-sized bed where I lay, and a pile of clothes, alarmingly colorful, lays folded on a wooden trunk at the end of the bed. Curtains cover the window, and the shadows of nighttime move beyond it.

So a house, then, and not some underground bunker where I'd have to worry about being crushed to death in a cave-in.

A quick check of limbs and lungs confirms that I'm better, but it still feels like I've been chewed up, swallowed, and squeezed out into a litter box.

"Tia…?"

Silence. It stretches into minutes. This silence pins me to the bed and forces a reflection that I usually manage to avoid, especially after such an exquisite failure as this.

In hindsight, what I did at that garden party was stupid.

The overconfidence I once accused the Redstones of was the same thing that brought me to this place. Wherever this place is.

Away from Mai.

At the thought of Mai, my entire body explodes with pain. Oh, because I just sat up like an idiot. A groan slips past my clenched teeth.

"Xóchitl! Lie still. You're still healing."

My Aunt Carmen appears at the door I didn't notice before. She looks worried, tired. The black blouse and slacks she wears a contrast to her sister's white dress. Her short hair looks a little crazed, like she's been running her fingers through it for hours.

"Mai. Where is she?" The trembling in my arms forces me back down to the pillow. "How long have I been here?"

"Almost two days. As for Mai, she's probably with her family." Aunt Ana follows slowly behind her sister, glowing in white. She floats to the foot of my bed like the angel of death. The touch of her hand through the thin blanket covering me is meant to be a comfort. But it only makes me more frantic to see Mai.

"What? We need to go get her." The blanket tangles in my legs and stops me from getting out of the bed. Exhausted from the brief struggle, I fall back against the pillow, gasping.

"You shouldn't have said that, Ana. That family is full of devils and no one is safe with them."

Tia Ana lightly squeezes my foot before settling in one of the chairs near the bed. "Devils belong with other devils."

"Mai isn't like them." The denial scrapes through my throat.

Mai is the opposite of what the Redstones stand for. She's fighting as Mercy because she wants to save the world. It's sweet. But it's also suicide.

Her mother would rather see her dead than waste her power saving humans.

"Whatever Mai Redstone is or isn't, isn't your concern right now, *cariño*." Tia Carmen tries to soothe me. "You have to give your body time to get better."

As usual, her sister doesn't let it go. "It would be easy for her to fall back into the good graces of her family. Sure, she talks about hating them, but I'm sure she feels perfectly safe with them. She hasn't lost like you've lost because of them."

"You're right, Tia," I tell her through teeth clenched in pain. "Her control over her body was taken away from her—"

"And your whole life was taken away from you." Tia Ana's hands land on her hips.

My head begins to pound. "I'm not going to compare trauma, Tia. Mai and I have both lost because of the Redstones. I won't let them take us, too." My stomach muscles protest as I sit up, and I can't suppress a gasp of agony.

Dammit. How off my game was I to let those Redstones get the best of me?

"God! Stop riling her up, Ana!" Tia Carmen rests a hand in the center of my chest with a shushing sound. "It's okay, love."

Slowly, warmth radiates from her fingers and into my body. I hiss from the pain of suddenly falling back into the bed but then, just as quickly, the aches begin to fade. So does my clear thinking.

"Rest, Xóchitl." Her voice is firm. "If anybody is going to break you tonight, it's not us. You're here to heal not make yourself worse."

But it's like she's speaking from far away. Vaguely, I'm aware of Tia Ana leaving the room after saying something about tea.

My tongue feels too heavy to speak, but I give it a good try, fighting against my aunt's attempts at shutting my brain down.

"Tia, stop. I can't be spaced out right now. I need to find Mai and finish this shit I started with her family."

"Stop growling at me and lay down. Don't let me set Ana on you. She'll really knock you out and you won't like it. Or maybe that's exactly what I should do to settle you down."

"No!" That's not what I want. That's not what I need. I need to be clearheaded. I need to think. I need to plan.

My eyes want to drift shut again, but I open them wide and push hard at the sensation of drowsiness. Tia Carmen frowns but doesn't try to put me to sleep again.

A gentle tap of bare feet against hardwood floors announce Tia Ana's return. With a sharp look in my direction, she sets a mug of something hot on the bedside table.

"Rest, Xóchitl." She nudges her sister out of the way, then takes a spoon wrapped in a cloth napkin from her pocket. "No arguments. And if I see you trying to leave, the next thing you know you'll be tied up in this bed and not for any reason that you'll like."

Now, this is just weird. "Tia!"

"Exactly." A sharp smile flits across her face. "I have a thousand ways to torture you and making inappropriate comments about your sex life is just one of them. Keep squirming around at your own peril."

Then, after helping me sit up, she slowly feeds me the concoction in the mug. It's warm and smells like ginger. The taste isn't as pleasant.

When the cup is empty, she pats my shoulder with a teasing "Good girl," then leaves the room.

Once she's gone, Tia Carmen pulls the blanket up to my shoulders and reclaims her seat. Whatever Ana has forced on me suffuses my whole body in warmth and calm.

"How did you find me?"

"My crazy sister, of course." My tia rolls her eyes. "She's wanted to come visit you since the day you left. At home, if she isn't talking about how you abandoned us, she's plotting to surprise you with a kidnapping back to Mexico." It's obvious she's not joking.

"Then a few days ago, she comes into my room with plane tickets. Says we're going to see you and will stay at a hotel if necessary, though she hopes you haven't lost your home training enough to let that happen."

Her barb hits its intended target and I flinch. Though the apartment is Mai's, not technically mine, my tias are welcome any place where I am. "You know I'd never let that happen, Tia."

She waves a dismissive hand. "Anyway, when we arrived, there was something foul in the air. I could just about taste it as soon as we landed. Ana knows people here, if you can believe that. So she asked her friend who picked us up from the airport to go straight to you. We barely stepped out of the car before Ana heard something."

Tia Ana has really fantastic hearing. It's cost me a few secrets over the years.

"I wanted to rush right in, but she stopped me. We waited barely a minute before we saw you flying out to meet us. But not the way we dreamed. We picked you off the sidewalk, put you in the car, and drove away."

Thank all the gods they came when they did. The idea of bleeding out on the sidewalk or, worse, ending up in a human hospital didn't exactly make me want to jump for joy.

"Where exactly is 'here'?" I coughed to clear the tremor from my voice.

"Honestly, I have no idea. But Ana says it's safe. And you know I believe my sister when it comes to things like that."

Unlike Carmen, Ana has always been interested in enforcers and the job we do. She asks endless questions and speculates out loud about the things that my mother got into. If my aunt's power had been interesting or useful enough, she would have signed up to be an enforcer, too. But the power she has, although impressive, isn't aggressive enough for what the enforcers need. We have some healers with us, but only those who also harm with their ability.

"I'm relieved you both found me. I don't know where I'd be if it wasn't for you."

"Dead."

I heal fast, but she's probably right. "So now that I'm not dead and Mai is still with her family, what's the big plan?"

"For you to rest just a little while longer." She clasps her hands in her lap and gives me a firm look.

"Tia, I don't have time. Mai doesn't have time."

"Somehow, I knew you'd say that."

At a single touch of her hand to my forehead, weakness invades me like a poison. "No…" But there's nothing I can do about the heaviness in my head and in my limbs.

"Sleep, love. You'll feel much stronger when you wake. I promise."

Her words are already drifting away. Or am I the one drifting? My eyelids shutter my view of the small dark room, and sleep crashes over me like a tidal wave.

CHAPTER 23

AN INSISTENT VIBRATION FROM MY arm drags me out of a deeper than normal sleep. The vibration is familiar, and urgent. *Work.* Instantly, I'm awake.

Aches and pains ladder up and down my body as I sit up and shove aside the blanket, but none of that matters. Heartbeat banging in my chest, I read the digital text on the bracelet that never comes off.

> *Ethan Redstone escaped. We need your team now.*

Redstone. This is worse than anything I could've imagined. I knew keeping him locked up like a pet was a bad idea. What were the justiciars thinking, allowing him to sit there and plot a way out of the low-security jail?

Unless they wanted him to have an easy means of escape.

No. I can't afford to give that thought any more room to grow. Betrayals are an everyday possibility in Meta life, but not from us. Not from this part of our society that's always been separate from the mess of politics and backstabbing. Right?

The muscles and aches in my body pull as I stand up. My head wobbles on my neck like an oversized blossom on a stalk.

Breathe. You can't afford to be weak. Not right now.

In. Out. The breaths move through my lungs, deep and easy. My feet stay steady under me. Mostly.

Footsteps slap against the tile floors, and my tias rush in.

"Xóchitl!" Tia Carmen stares at me in horror.

A LOVER'S MERCY

Tia Ana grabs my arm. Her grip is gentle but firm. "Where on earth are you going?"

"I have to get to work." I shrug off the hold and stagger toward the pile of clothes I noticed earlier.

"You're not in any shape to work. Either at that school or with your enforcers."

"I don't have a choice." The jeans in the pile are thankfully plain, but the T-shirt is a blinding tie-dye. "Hopefully these are for me." The jeans scrape my bruised and aching thighs, but they fit well enough not to fall off my hips. "Because I'm taking them."

Tia Ana steps in front of me. She doesn't try to touch me this time.

"Why don't you just teleport to wherever your uniform is? Isn't that better than walking around looking colorblind?"

Our eyes meet. She knows.

Earlier, as soon as I woke up in this room, I tried to teleport and couldn't. My power was drained completely from what I'd been through with the Redstones. I can stand upright and dress myself, but the space inside me where my power lay is a gaping wound.

"I can't," I confess.

Tia Ana curses. "You're being foolish." She touches me again, and the sensation of power from her fingers is immediate.

"Don't!" Flinching back, I almost topple over, but her hand doesn't leave my skin. "I can't function with anything from you guys in my system."

"It's not that. You've made your decision. I'm giving you a little extra to help out until you're back at a hundred percent." She pulls her hand away, suddenly looking drained. Her cheekbones look sharper, and her hair looks gray now instead of the usual lustrous silver.

That's when I feel the difference. A blush of power under my skin that's different from my own. It's warm, like the heat of an afternoon sun seeping up from the sidewalk and into bare feet. A light top-up. It's not enough to help me stop a beast like Ethan Redstone, but it will at least keep me upright and moving forward.

"Tia, I don't know what to say." I grasp her hands in mine. They feel unbearably fragile.

"Don't say a damn thing. Just get to work and come back to us safe."

Tia Carmen's hand rests on my back. "Don't die."

"I'll do my best."

Two of the three women I love most in the world hold on to me fiercely, their eyes bright with moisture. Then they let me go.

"We'll see you soon."

The air in the small room is warm, a comforting blanket over the anxiety of my thundering heartbeat, the worry for Mai, and everything else that's blown my calm to pieces. Tia Carmen and Ana grip me tight, and the touch of their hands sears me deep. An uncomfortable heat glows behind my eyes, and I squeeze them tight to stop any betraying wetness from falling.

This won't be the last time I see my tias. It can't be.

"Yes, I'll see you soon." Then I tap my bracelet.

The channel opens immediately. "Go ahead, Commander."

My tias step back and put their arms around each other's waists. Moisture glows in their eyes.

"I need transport assist," I say, firming my voice and my spine. At work, I can't afford to be weak.

"Immediate?"

"Yes."

"Stand by."

The connection ends. "Thanks for the juice, Tia. I promise not to waste it."

Tia Ana rolls her eyes. "That's the last thing I'm worried a—"

Cold clamps around me as my sick room, my tias, and the small respite I had from all the bullshit disappears.

"What's the status?" I snap as soon as the war room appears in all its stark, electronics-heavy glory.

For a split second, there's only silence. Except for Pascale and Farr, the room is empty. They both stare like I've just popped in stark naked. Sure, I look rough and a little ridiculous in the tie-dye, but still.

Farr snaps out of it first. "Ah… On his way to the visitors' room, Redstone got out of his stasis cuffs and took off. Not sure exactly how it happened, but the end result is that the bastard is gone."

My team is all business, but the knowledge that Redstone is my woman's cousin, and a danger to her, simmers between all of us. A muscle tics in my jaw.

Ethan Redstone is in the wind. Shit.

The plain fact is our facility isn't meant to be a prison. Temporary holding is just that. It wouldn't take long for someone to figure out a way to escape. A powerful Meta like Ethan Redstone should've been kept sedated most of the time and given a damn catheter and feeding tube, not asking for potty breaks and complaining about the food.

"All right." I fight back a sigh. "Any leads on where he's gone?"

"That's where you come in," Pascale says, though he stares hard at my baggy jeans and vision-destroying T-shirt, as surprised as Farr.

"Are you all right?" Farr comes right out and asks. "You look like shit."

"If I ever need my ego stroked, I know where not to come," I tell her, dry as the dessert. But a shivery pain in my side confirms her unprofessional opinion.

"Incoming," Pascale announces seconds before Caleb steps out of nothing and into the room. His uniform is on, and he's ready to work.

"What's the situation with Redstone?" Caleb asks, gaze sweeping over everyone in the room. If I didn't smell the sex on him, I'd assume we just got him out of his living room armchair from a morning of TV watching. He's more prepared than I am.

My shoulder twinges with a distant pain. "Give me a sec."

There's a small door to the larger office that leads to the storage locker containing everything we usually need: clean uniforms, weapons, energy bars for long days or hours on the road. I slip into the locker and, as quickly as my healing body will allow, change into a spare uniform and grab some supplies, including a gun. When I get back to the room, Caleb is settled into a chair next to Farr and discussing a plan of attack.

I keep going like I never left the room. "I'd assume Redstone went back to Atlanta. Maybe not the house where he lived but definitely an area close to his family and allies. He has somebody trying to prove his innocence."

Pascale snorts. "Innocence. Right." He passes me a tablet with the report on Ethan's escape.

"Exactly what I think." I quickly look through the information. "But his little helper caused a lot of damage out there."

Caleb eyes the bruises on my face. "Need some help with that?"

Briefly, I think of telling them what happened at the Redstone garden party but remember there's no such thing as privacy here. The walls have ears, and I'm not in the mood to share with that many people. "No. At least not yet, but I might later on."

Farr looks up from the data on the large screen she's sharing with Caleb. "Maybe we can kill two birds with one stone."

She has a point. I nod sharply and turn to Pascale. "What else do we know?"

He pulls up the computer imagery on the largest screen for all of us to see. It takes up the entire front wall.

In the video, Redstone sits in his cell, acting listless and resigned when the two enforcers come to take him to the visitors' room where Caressa is waiting for him. They have him out of his cell and standing between them for barely two seconds before he abruptly bends his wrists and the stasis cuffs pop open. By the time the cuffs clatter to the floor, Ethan is gone, teleported off to who knows where. It's fast and practiced. He didn't once hesitate.

"Shit," Caleb breathes out.

"That's one word for it." For years, my team and I have been trying to get the higher-ups to create an anti-port space out of the entire "prison," but they've always said it was unnecessary since we don't keep prisoners, only hold them for a very limited time. Another reasoning of theirs is that a change like that would force teleporting enforcers to move off-site to use their power. Well, I'd rather have to go someplace else to port out than risk a dangerous animal like Redstone running to freedom.

"What about Caressa Redstone?" I scan the report again just to verify that she isn't named other than being the reason Ethan was being moved from his cell.

"We don't have a thing on her," Pascale says. "When officers got to the visitor's area, she acted as surprised as any of them."

Farr taps something on her keyboard. "As soon as he disappeared from the facility, the computers noticed the unfamiliar shift signature and raised the alarm."

"How much lead time does he have on us?" I ask, though I could easily just check the time stamp on the video.

"Less than thirty minutes."

"Good." I look at my watch. "We'll need all the help we can get, especially since the family is going on the assumption that he's innocent and we're trying to frame him for someone else's murders."

"He tried to kill Mandaia Redstone's heir," Caleb says with a meaningful glance at me, his bad try at being subtle to avoid the cameras that record everything we do and say here. "He killed your sister. There's nothing innocent about this piece of garbage."

As if I need reminding. "Right. So let's go get him and quit wasting time."

A map of the Redstone mansion and grounds in Alpharetta goes up on the screen for everyone to quickly memorize. Then one of Caressa's condo and a few of the other places we suspect Redstone might try to hide.

"So back to the question Farr asked before." Pascale looks me up and down with a narrowed gaze. "You're not at a hundred percent, right?"

I become aware then of just how closely they're all listening for my response. Which they should be. We can't have relevant secrets on an operation.

"Correct." A sigh hisses from between my clenched teeth. "My strength is down by about half, and I can't teleport."

Pascale nods sharply. "But you can still find Redstone?"

"Yes. I would've said something if I couldn't." Maybe.

The brief moment of tension in the room dissipates. "Okay, now that you're done questioning me, let's get this job done." I squeeze Pascale's arm to let him know I'm not taking his questions personally. He's just doing his job as my second in command.

Farr and Caleb turn away from the monitor and give me their full attention at the same time that Pascale lets out an amused grunt of acknowledgment. Laid-back and easy once again, he waves a hand my way. "Okay, boss. What's the plan?"

Less than ten minutes later, everyone is briefed and ready—masks on, guns strapped to our thighs, and our utility belts fully stocked. We run a quick check of our shared mental link we only ever activate on stealth missions.

Ready? I check the team.

Yes, they each silently echo.

"Fantastic." Farr gives a full-on evil grin. "I have this new stasis collar I'm just dying to try."

"Don't get your hopes up. Escape from us means the capture is dead or alive." Caleb looks much too happy reminding us about this. His fingers tap restlessly against the buckle of his utility belt.

"My money is on dead." Pascale's gaze slips in my direction.

Yeah. Preferably with his bloody and beating heart in my clenched fist. Nobody hurts Mai and gets away with it. Not even me.

CHAPTER 24

WHERE IS ETHAN REDSTONE?

Because the simplest answer is usually the right one, we start with the Alpharetta house. Pascale ports us to the mansion, and immediately, the scent of flowers fills my nose. I breathe it quickly in to get used to it, then fan out the rest of the team, my internal radar on high alert for Redstone's unique signature.

The house is protected. Wards and traps of all types are meant to trip up any human or Meta trying to enter uninvited. We tear through their defenses like they're nothing but cobwebs.

Our boots are silent on the marble floors. I reach out all of my senses.

Only the Redstones are here. No maids. No personal assistants. Just the family—as if they had been expecting this moment with Ethan to come. A prodigal criminal returned to the den.

Right now is about work. Finding Ethan Redstone and getting him. But despite my focus, the first thing that jumps out at me is her. Mai. That brilliant ribbon of her consciousness is drifting through the halls of the large house like the most beautiful thing in the world.

Mai. My heart. Mine.

Focus.

Mai is with her parents. I sense them on the main level of the mansion along with Cayman and Abi. Caressa is here, too, but somewhere else in this large house. Very faintly, I hear her voice, the distinct tones that try for soothing with a touch of sensuality and just end up being annoying as fuck. But maybe I'm biased.

Ethan and Caressa are together. His overconfident tang is strong on the air, his particular stink from being in jail, remnants of his fear, and now triumph that he got away. Presumably, he's happy enough and, once he makes his presence known to the family, expects Mandaia Redstone to shelter him now that there is doubt about who he did or didn't murder in his spare time.

A growl rumbles through my chest as we prowl through the house.

"Chill, Commander," Pascale cautions. "We're not trying to get caught before we get to him. Remember that."

He's right. I swallow down that betraying growl of sound.

The team is silent, all the chatter taking place only between our minds as we move toward where the strong signature of Meta activity is.

Toward the salon. Up ahead. I gesture in that direction even though I don't need to. The people in the house, in the room, are making no effect at being quiet.

Should we just take them all? Bloodlust strums through Caleb like a pulsing, purple line.

He is even less forgiving than I am. Unlike me, his family is large and power poor. Over the years, he's seen how rich families like the Redstones have taken advantage of their position and stepped on people they considered beneath them. Through our link, I feel Caleb's focus and fury. He's ready to dismember Ethan Redstone and feast on his bones.

And I thought I'm the one a little out of control.

We're only here for Ethan, I tell Caleb for the second time tonight.

They're talking. Farr has hooked into all the electronics they carry with them. Cell phones and cameras. She has audio and visual.

Yes, they are.

Muting my awareness of the others on the team, I focus on what Farr is seeing and hearing.

The family is in the salon where Mai ended up the night I came here for dinner. From multiple cell-phone-camera angles, I see they're sitting in a loose circle. Mandaia, her husband, and Cayman sit many inches apart on the long, L-shaped leather sectional. In one of the green velvet armchairs, Abi sits picking at the edge of her thumbnail. Mai is in the other armchair, sitting rigidly with her hands clamped to the chair's rounded arms.

It looks like she can barely move.

Vines the thickness of her thighs bind her tightly to the chair. Two of them wind around her belly and biceps, and one latches each foot to the chair's. Since the last time I saw her, she's changed into short boots, jeans, and a tank top. The vines press into her bare arms but somehow leave the skin smooth and untouched.

This is her mother's work.

The corners of her mouth are tight and unyielding, and fury pours out of her in a steady, hot stream. Her sadness blankets the room like a summer heat in Georgia.

She's here. They didn't hurt her.

The feeling of relief is so intense that I stagger and bump into a nearby pedestal.

"Fuck!" Standing just behind me, Pascal catches the porcelain vase on top of the pedestal before it can fall to the floor.

I curse myself as we all freeze.

Cayman's head jerks up. "What was that noise?"

"What noise?" Abi leaves off mutilating her finger. "Are you being paranoid again?"

"I'm not being paranoid." He jumps to his feet and heads for the closed door. "We just killed another Meta, and her body disappeared before we could do anything with it. What you call paranoid, I call careful."

Quinn Redstone makes a tired motion in the air. "Sit down, Cayman."

"But Dad—"

"Sit. Down." Exhaustion drags at his father's face. "We don't have time for any more of your theatrics." Actually, they all look tired, like they've been sitting around like this, talking or whatever, since they almost killed me two days ago.

Only Mandaia, in her unexpected jeans and white blouse, looks fresh and unbothered. With a nonchalant crossing of her legs, she fixes Mai with a cool glance.

"Daughter mine, I can't keep you safe unless you tell me the truth about what's been going on."

"Safe?" Mai gives her mother a dirty look. "By making me your prisoner?" Growling, she jerks her restrained body hard enough that the vines around her creak and the chair jerks across the wooden floor.

"You're safer here with us than out in the world, Mandaia-Pili." Mandaia sighs like she's talking to a particular stubborn child. Which in her mind, she is. "You got yourself involved with a killer, Mai. You don't think the enforcers will come after you as some sort of accessory and throw you in the cell next to Ethan?"

"No, I don't."

A look of cunning gleams Mandaia's amber eyes. "Then you must know something we don't. What is it, Mai?"

A muscle clenches in Mai's jaw when she clamps her mouth shut. Her mind is shut tight, but the pain she feels eddies around her like a river of blood. "Let me go, Mother. That's *all* I have to say to you right now."

My heart feels like a pulpy mess in the cage of my chest. I can't listen to any more of this. Abruptly disconnecting from the conversation in the salon, I slip into Farr's feed to see exactly where Ethan is hiding.

He's close.

High in one of the upper rooms of the large house, arguing with Caressa. The feed from the smart TV that Farr has tapped into shows everything. In the short time he's been out of jail, Redstone managed to have a shower and otherwise clean up. In pressed gray slacks and a white button-down shirt, he looks like he just left work on casual Friday instead of a prison cell. He still looks like a wild animal.

And Caressa is the one who's been helping him. She doesn't seem pleased with the results of her plotting, though.

"Why did you come here, Ethan?" She stalks back and forth in front of Redstone who's sitting in an armchair like a king on his throne. The ruffled edges of her blouse flutter with every step. "I told you, it's not time yet. I'm working on a plan. Some powerful friends of mine are putting the pressure on Mandaia to support you. That's why we got this far. You weren't supposed to leave that jail!"

Her usually calm façade is in tatters.

Ethan smooths an invisible wrinkle from the knee of his slacks. "I'm sick of your 'not yet.' No way was I going to sit in that hole a second longer waiting for your slow-ass plans to take shape."

Caressa's tennis shoes slap the rug in front of Ethan's chair as she makes another circuit of the small room. "Well, I hope you're sick of being free, too. What you've done just ruined our best chance of getting you completely exonerated. It's easier to believe you're innocent and ready to be released if you're actually in jail, Ethan." Caressa stops suddenly, her hands clenched at her sides. "Do you think the justiciar will listen to you now that you broke out and ran?"

The leather armchair creaks as Ethan slowly sits back, his gaze glittering. "First of all, that's not how you talk to me, Caressa." His growl is menacing enough for the woman to snap her mouth shut. But she also looks a little turned on.

Jesus.

Disgusted, I pull back from the feed of Ethan and his acolyte.

Let's port up there, grab Ethan and Caressa, then go, I project to the team. *After we're done here, we can bring charges against the family for aiding a Meta murderer.*

Good. Caleb unsnaps the holster holding his gun then snaps it again. "We can take him down and get back to our lives. This idiot ruined my night more than enough."

Wait. Farr's command sends a warning jolt through all of us. We know to pay attention when she uses that tone. We can all see it, the way her brain is working with the flicker of her eyes. *We should see where this is going. Ethan is here and obviously this Caressa chick is part of the plan. But we need to see where the rest of the family stands before we act. If they're not part of this, the justiciar needs to know. Revenge is not our mission here.*

If a mental voice could point a finger, that's exactly what hers is doing.

You're right. Let's be thorough and clear about where they are with Ethan. As much as I hate the Redstones, I can't argue against this. Yes, they almost killed me, but for Mai's sake, I'm willing to see their actions as reactionary instead of malicious. If they didn't help Ethan escape.

As for the family, it just looks like some good old-fashioned in-fighting going on, Farr projects. *They don't know Ethan is here. Doesn't even seem like they're expecting him.*

Okay. I shift my attention back to what's happening with Ethan and Caressa. *Farr, you stay here and keep your eye on that situation and let me know when* you *think I should move on Ethan.*" I try to keep the sarcasm out of my voice. And almost succeed.

Pascale laughs at me, because what else would he do? *Keep your pants on, boss.*

I am *the boss. Try to remember that.*

As if you'd let us forget. The amusement in Farr's voice sends an answering ripple through the rest of the team. Jackasses.

Grabbing me and Caleb, Pascale ports us off to where Ethan and Caressa are playing out their little drama. We appear just outside the closed door, but I keep most of my attention on the audio and video feeds coming from inside the room.

"Fine, Ethan. I apologize." Hands clasped in front of her and with her mouth a vulnerable curve, Caressa looks down at the still seated Ethan. "I stand by what I said even though I should have said it a different way."

What is it about otherwise intelligent women and assholes?

"It's all right. We're both a little stressed right now." Ethan takes Caressa's hand in his and brushes his lips over her knuckles, probably her reward for still standing by him through this whole farce. "Let's go down and tell the family what's going on. Once they realize all that shit the enforcers said about me was made up, they'll have no problem going to the tribunal and telling them I'm innocent."

Denial is a hell of a drug.

"Okay, good. That's the whole reason you came here anyway." Caressa nods like she's about to run and tell the rest of the family to accept Ethan because he's sorry, cross his heart and hope Mai dies.

I want to shake her until her empty head falls off.

With Caleb and Pascale by my side, I wait, the three of us paying attention to the feed from the digital devices in the room as well as the real world around us. I feel my power coming back, at least some of it with my Tia's help. I push, *gently*, just to test it. But that part of me remains dormant. I can't teleport yet.

My body's betraying weakness makes me want to break something.

"They have to accept what I saw, especially since it's obvious I was set up," Ethan says, still holding Caressa's hand.

"You're right, Ethan," Caressa eagerly agrees. "If it comes down to it, I'll make sure they accept the truth."

Because they can't see me, I roll my eyes.

Calmer than he was before, Caleb huffs out a silent laugh.

In the room, Caressa takes a deep breath and gives Ethan a reassuring smile. The idiot. "Okay, let's go."

Then he takes her hand and ports away.

They just ported out, I tell Farr. *Heading your way.*

Pascale winks out in a rush of cold. *They're here*, Pascale says a moment later. *Right outside the room with the family.*

Farr laughs without amusement. *They're actually about to knock like polite murderers.*

Let's just let this play out like you said, I tell Farr. *See what this family is up to.*

A good strategy, Farr agrees to her own plan with a laugh.

Such a comedian. *I'm on my way down there.*

Pascale appears. *Want a lift?*

These guys I work with are so funny. It just kills me.

We appear at the same level as the family meeting, and through the eyes of a nearby security camera, I can see what Farr said about

Ethan. He lifts a confident hand and knocks on the door as the team and I watch.

The voices inside the room rise and fall with confusion.

"Who's that?"

"I told you I heard something."

"What's going on?"

After a few seconds of hesitation, Cayman opens the door. "It's Ethan," he says in an overly loud voice, and everyone in the room behind him falls silent.

"What's going on?" Through the cell camera, I see Abi stand and try to look past her brother.

Cayman gives a brief shake of his head and steps aside for Ethan to walk in.

Stand by, team. My hand tightens on my holstered weapon.

Standing by, they each echo.

In the room, Mai's family is tense and watchful as Ethan saunters in with Caressa just behind him, like a good lackey. No one speaks. The door closes.

"You need to leave here. Now." Abi stands in front of Mai with her arms crossed.

Her mother extends a gentling hand in Abi's direction. "What's going on here, Ethan?" Mandaia's gaze is neutral as she leans back in the sofa, but the cameras pick up the slight tension in her arms. The leg she so casually crossed before is now uncrossed and firmly on the ground. "Why aren't you still in prison?"

In her chair, Mai tenses up, the muscles bared in her tank top bunching and releasing. Abi stands in front of her still, a fierce, if cute, guard dog.

"Didn't Caressa tell you?" Ethan's smile is confident as he approaches his powerful aunt. "I'm innocent."

Abi makes a disgusted noise. "I sincerely hope you don't really believe that, Ethan."

"I'm not the Absolution Killer," Ethan says. "I've been trying to tell you since they dragged me off to that hell hole."

"Caressa told us Xóchitl was really the one who killed Uncle Stephen and tried to frame you." The tone of Abi's voice is... interesting.

"What, you don't believe Caressa or me?" He lifts his head to stare down at Abi.

"I tend not to believe assholes who try to kill my sister."

"Aunt Mandaia and everyone else believed Caressa enough at the time to kill that murdering bitch, Xóchitl."

A sharp breath leaves Mai's bared teeth. If looks could kill, Ethan would be a slab of cooling meat right now.

"Or at least they tried to kill her." Abi's words are a quiet whisper, but everyone else heard her anyway.

"What do you mean 'tried'?" Caressa jumps in.

"There's no proof she's really dead," Abi says. "And when you ran down to where you'd supposedly tossed her body, there was nothing there."

Mai's body jerks hard in the chair. The air around her crackles with dangerous energy I can feel even from the other side of the door. "You didn't tell me that!"

Still keeping a wary eye on Ethan, Abi steps back to rest a hand on Mai's shoulder. "I don't need to. That...that connection you and she have? If she's alive, you know it. From the way you've been sitting there and acting like you're helpless, it's obvious you're playing games with Mom and Cayman, trying to figure out if they know where Xóchitl is." Abi's hand clenches on Mai's shoulder. "You can't afford to wait anymore. You have to do something!"

All eyes in the room jump to Mai.

"She's not strong enough to get out of those binds," Cayman mutters with a laugh.

"What do you know about any of this, Abi?" Mandaia demands at the same time.

"Nothing. Only that Mai loves this woman and you...you take Caressa's word and her sketchy recording as fact for something none of us really have any proof of and you tried to kill Xóchitl. The enforcers are going to rip you apart for that, by the way."

"We're going to explain to them what happened," Caressa says gently. She links her fingers in front of her, looking at everyone in the room, her lips curved up in a benign half-smile. Her power. She's working them, influencing them. "They can't fault us for taking our own justice after theirs goes wrong."

"But how could you do that to Mai?" Abi blinks and rubs at her forehead, like she's only half-aware of what she's doing, fighting off Caressa's influence. Her eyes narrow and she throws an accusing look at her mother. "How could you turn against your own daughter like that? Am I next?"

Mandaia ignores Abi. "I repeat, Ethan. You should not be here. The family did what we were…strongly encouraged to. We spoke at your trial." She exchanges a quick look with her husband who gives her a small nod of support.

What the Twilight Zone is going on here?

"Now go wait for whatever judgment the justiciars will mete out," Mandaia finishes.

"I will not!" Ethan's voice rises to a shout. Hands shoved in his pockets, he leans forward, his chin a sharp aggression. "Waiting for them to deliver the same so-called justice is just stupid. Family sticks together and that's what I want you to do for me now."

"Absolutely not." For the first time, Quinn Redstone speaks. "You're not in a position to make demands, Ethan. Not one. If it wasn't for you and your father, this family wouldn't be in this position."

When did he finally start feeling his balls?

Everything happened to his daughter under his watch, and not once did he lift a finger to help her. What suddenly changed?

"Get out of here, Ethan," Mai's father continues, his voice low and deep and scathing. "And even if they do find you not guilty, you're not welcome back in this house."

Both Ethan and Caressa wear identical expressions of shock, as if they just watched the statues at Mount Rushmore peel away from the rocks and start doing the moonwalk. I probably have the same look on my face.

"I think my husband has made the family's position perfectly clear, Ethan." Mandaia looks supremely unbothered by her nephew's outburst. The flowering plants hanging from the ceiling don't seem so relaxed, though. They quiver with a palpable energy as if they're just waiting to strangle someone with their snaking vines.

After a quick look at his father, then Mandaia, Cayman stands with his arms crossed, eyeing Ethan and Caressa like all he needs is a flimsy excuse of a reason to throw them out. Bouncer-come-lately.

"Ethan, please leave," Abi says again. "If Mom and Dad don't call the enforcers, I will."

"No." Ethan softens his expression, but his hands have turned into fists inside his pants pockets. He's not stupid enough to walk close to his Aunt Mandaia, though. "I came here to prove my innocence and that's exactly what I'm going to do. Caressa convinced you to speak at my trial. Come and do it again, and bring more of your high-powered friends this time. I'm a Redstone. That means something."

Quinn Redstone makes a rough noise. "Yes, it means that one of the most powerful families on the continent has a tumor growing inside it that needs to be cut out. It means you're a weakness we can't afford."

"No, I keep telling you. It's not that." Caressa's voice is a soft and convincing murmur. She must be off her game and nervous if she's being so obvious about using her influence. "If you keep it quiet that Ethan has been accused of doing...things, then none of the other families will ever know. We'll get to keep the reputation we have, and Ethan will be safe."

"To keep on killing and violating people he thinks are weaker than him, just like this father." Mai speaks up for the first time. "Yes, I'm sure the other families will respect us so much for that. The weak in need of protection will just rush to join us."

An animal-like rumble leaves Ethan's throat. "The weak have no place in this family!"

"*You* have no place in this family!" Wicked blades erupt along Mai's arms and all down the side of her body, ripping into the chair's soft fabric. The blades effortlessly slash through the thick vines holding her captive, and she jumps up from what's left of her chair. It clatters against the floor, sounding like a gunshot.

Her sudden freedom is like a dash of ice water on the room. Her sister leaps away from her with a sharp cry while her parents jerk to their feet, eyeing her with caution.

Ethan, though, has never been the brightest crayon in the pack. Growling low, he launches himself across the room at Mai.

CHAPTER 25

WE'VE HEARD ENOUGH. I SLIP from my hiding place in the room next to the salon. *Take Redstone down now.*

My foot slams against the salon door, and the woods cracks hard, the door flying inward with a crash. The thud under my boot is satisfying after listening helplessly while the Redstones talk over their damn issues.

For precious seconds, the family freezes in place.

"Ethan Redstone, you're under arrest," I say. "If you choose to come with me of your own free will, it'll be much better for you than if I have to drag your ass out of here by your hair."

Farr instantly slips into the salon, her gun drawn and pointed at Ethan.

"So, we're going in now, then?" Sarcasm twists her lips.

I ignore her. Caleb and Pascale rush in behind me just as Ethan's porting tell flashes in my mind. Before he can shift out, I grab him and blanket him with my own porting power.

My hold isn't gentle. Fingers digging into him hard enough to creak the leather of my gloves. The fury rides me hot and hard, and a red haze wavers in front of my eyes as I slam him into the floor. My breath heaves. My heart gallops hard in my ribcage.

"Leave him alone!" Caressa's shout threatens to blast out my eardrums.

"Mai!" Abi cries out, but I don't waste valuable seconds looking for them.

With Ethan contained, Caleb and Pascale crowd the Redstones on one side of the room, while Farr grabs Caressa with gloved hands.

I'm vaguely aware of Mandaia and Cayman being handcuffed and shoved to safety behind pieces of furniture.

Ethan's little minion is talking, something in that annoyingly soothing voice of hers that's intended to trick. Not all of us are immune.

"Gag her!" I shout.

Under me, Ethan twists over onto his back and tries to port out again. My hold on him falters moments before he growls in triumph. A kick slams into my stomach, and I nearly scream from the agony.

"Stay still!" I want to break him, but the trembling in my arms and back warns me that this thought is only a dream. My body is weaker than it's ever been, and the strength of my will doesn't make up for it.

The power my tia lent me isn't as strong as my own, and I feel its failings with every punch Ethan lands on my body.

"Not as strong as you think, are you?" Before I can recover, he jabs me in the kidney. I double over, the bile rushing up in my throat in a hot and bitter flood.

Suddenly, he's off me and Mai is there, her grip stronger than mine, but I know she won't be able to keep him. He's still trying to phase out, and my power alone is too weak to keep him here. I exchange the grip on one arm for the other, hard and fast while Mai slams her arm into his throat.

"Don't kill him," I growl at her only to have her look at me like I'm crazy.

Mai smiles widely, all teeth and shimmering eyes. *I can't believe you're here.* She slides the thought into my mind as smooth as honey even while she still pants and grapples with Ethan. My whole being melts, but I won't risk paying any attention to her now. I've never been any good at multitasking.

"Pascale!" I call out to my second in command. "Redstone is trying to port out. I can't hold him!"

Pascale rushes over to where Mai and I are trying to deal with Ethan, and the three of us struggle with him, all grunting with the effort.

Damn. Has he always been this strong?

No, I'm just too weak to properly fight him, dammit.

"Don't hurt him!" Even under the stati-cloth someone slapped over Caressa's mouth, I can hear her. She's seriously getting on my nerves.

Then she yelps as Caleb drags her back across the room with the other Redstones and pulls enhanced zip-ties tight around her wrists. We must be out of cuffs.

"Caressa, fight them!" Ethan growls, and I slam an elbow into his face for his trouble.

This kind of shit is beneath us. Brawling with some child killer like we're equals in the streets? This needs to be over, and soon. But the elbow jab took the last of my strength. I'm too weak to do more than gasp commands, and with Pascale there to prevent Ethan from porting out, I slowly back away from the fight, a hand pressed to the sharp pain in my stomach.

"Xóchitl. Is that you?" Abi is nearby and asking questions I can't answer. *How the hell can she figure that out through my mask?* I don't even look her way.

But at the sound of her voice, Ethan, who is rabidly fighting Pascale and Mai like he'd sooner die on the floor of his family home than go back to prison, looks up. His animal eyes latch onto me, and I feel the moment that he must see the resemblance that Abi just noticed.

Shit.

A look of wild joy flashes across his face, like his Christmas came early. "That is your little fuck toy, isn't it, Mai?"

I feel the ripple of shock from the other Redstones.

That's right, bitches. I'm not that easy to kill.

Quick as a cat, he rams a fist into Pascale's throat, and the sound of it is like a tile shattering. Pascale screams, an agonized sound, and Ethan twists away from Mai and arrows straight for me.

He slams into me like a battering ram, and my whole body blooms with pain. I gasp, biting back a shout. He can't win this. We can't let him.

Kept at bay by Caleb's scowl-threatening presence, his big gun, and the power-draining cuffs on their wrists, the rest of the family is forced to stay out of the way as the fight destroys the room. Lamps. The couch. All their pretty things.

Ethan is good. I remember it from before. Hard to forget the way he fights. His father, with his telekinesis, was a lazy fighter, relying on his mind to do all the work for him while letting his body grow weak and unable to defend himself in a fight. But Ethan never allowed himself that luxury of the truly powerful.

With his ability to phase gone under the tight grip of my arm, he's a beast, ferocious and skilled. I feel the blood bubble up through the rips in my skin. Bruises bloom. The bones rattle under my skin.

"I'm going to take your bitch from you the same way you stole my father from me." Ethan savagely tears into me.

It doesn't take a genius to figure out who he's talking about. And barely a breath later, he's on me, an arm tight under my throat and his fist slamming into my stomach over and over again.

The pain is blinding. I can't breathe. Everything from my neck down to my belly feels like a raw, pulsing mess.

"Get off her!" Mai throws him off me, and I gasp, sprawled on my back and desperately sucking in the suddenly available oxygen.

Oh God. Air. It feels incredible.

With her gun gripped in both hands, Farr drops to her knees at my side. "Commander, can you function?"

What the hell is she doing? Redstones first, me later.

"Yes!" I manage to gasp out. "Don't worry about me. Secure Caressa and make sure Redstone doesn't get away." The air rushing through my throat hurts. *God damn, it hurts.* "Then go to Pascale."

After a quick mental check to make sure I'm not hiding any lasting injuries, she's gone. But damn, the pain juddering through me isn't allowing me to move quite yet.

"Ethan Redstone, don't move!" Farr points the gun at Ethan, but even she isn't good enough to hit him and not hurt Mai in the process. "Shit!"

She dances around them, looking for a decent shot as they whirl in a blur of fists and flying legs and bared teeth. Ethan is trying to get the best of Mai, punching and kicking one moment, then twisting away to avoid the slashing sharpness of her claws the next.

"Mai!" Abi screams suddenly, and Mai jerks her head to look at her sister.

That's when Ethan strikes, a cobra showing his fangs. Still on my back and panting for breath, I see the blade a split second before I realize what it is. An enhanced metal that can cut through literally anything pitted against it. It gleams faintly pink in Ethan's underhanded grip.

"He's got a knife!" But my warning comes from a bruised throat, barely loud enough to be heard. I try again, this time with my thoughts. *Don't let him cut you.*

But I'm not sure if she hears me.

From the way Mai surges forward, I know she thinks this knife is just like any other. The blade slashes down.

"Farr!" But, suddenly, the enforcer is frozen in place, her gun pointed at Ethan but hanging uselessly from her hands.

Caressa? Is she the one doing this?

Mai's body jerks from the ram of the knife into her side.

"Mai!" A booming shout rattles everything in the room. Mandaia.

From a distance, I hear the groan and crack of terracotta pots, the wild shiver of leaves, vines hissing against each other as Mandaia tries to break free of her cuffs.

"Oh!" Ethan grins and stabs her again.

No. No. No. No.

Although it hurts like hell, I roll to my hands and knees. Redstone's not taking another thing from me. With a quick, jerking move that feels like I'm being split open, I'm there in front of Ethan, grabbing his knife hand that's ready to slash down into Mai once again. A surge of power blasts through me and I grip him tight, stopping him from porting away. He growls under me, trying to buck me off.

At the same time, I feel a power, Caressa's, trying to hold and direct me. I shrug her off.

Then the smell of cut grass explodes in the room. Something makes me look up in time to see a potted orchid hurling itself from the ceiling. Before I can move, it rushes past my face with the sensation of a swift breeze and smashes into Ethan's head. Ethan shouts out in shock, in pain. The pot explodes. Dirt. Purple blossoms. Shattered terracotta everywhere. His eyes roll back in his head. He sags underneath me like an abandoned marionette and passes out.

Silence.

Across the room, Mandaia stares at Ethan with burning eyes. Her chest is heaving, her teeth bared.

Heart racing with relief, I feel for the pulse in Ethan's neck. It's there. He's alive. That's all the thought I can spare for him now.

"Pascale!" It takes him longer than usual to appear at my side. Probably had something to do with his nearly shattered throat. "Get Mai to a healer. Now!"

A river of red surrounds Mai. Her lashes flutter against her cheeks as she fights to keep her eyes open. Blood pumps between the fingers she has pressed to her stomach. My hand tightens on Ethan's neck. He doesn't move.

"No… Don't!—" Even though that horse is long out of the barn, I can see Mai clench her teeth to stop herself from saying my name.

Pascale's hand appears on her shoulder, ready to take her away. Mai's flickering gaze meets mine. This is what Ethan's done. I can't let this go. Not this time.

What the hell is Pascale waiting for? He scoops her into his arms, and the blood pulses from Mai's belly. My name leaks from her lips, and she shakes her head.

She's telling me not to do it. Not to lay my murderous soul bare in front of my team and her family. But what I can't do is let Redstone escape only to come back to hurt her again.

"I'm a killer, baby." My words are a confession, a claiming of myself. "Not a superhero." Then I slash his throat.

Mai's face is agony, but I can feel the rush of relief from her as Ethan Redstone's life pours out over my hands in dark shades of red. A moment later, Pascale disappears with her in his arms.

Gradually, I become aware of my pained gasps, loud in the otherwise silent room. Except for Mandaia, the Redstones gawk at me. Corralled together in their shock, they blink at Ethan's cooling body and its blood pouring out around me. Mandaia, though, stares at the spot where Pascale disappeared with Mai.

My heart is the roar trapped inside a seashell.

Agony twitches through my muscles.

Then it recedes.

Slowly, I close my eyes. The world tilts, and I'm falling sideways into the already-drying blood.

CHAPTER 26

THE SOUND OF A JULIO Iglesias song, something about a moonlight lady, ripples from the kitchen and down the hall along with Tia Ana's terrible singing voice.

"I don't think that's how the song goes, sister!" Tia Carmen's laughter spills out with the clang of something metallic falling into the sink.

A riot of scents from the tamales they're making spices the air in Mai's condo and makes my mouth water. The best Sunday morning I've had in a long time. Breakfast was barely an hour ago, but the smell of the tamales jumpstarts my appetite all over again.

Or as much as anything of mine can be jumpstarted while I'm flat on my back on the couch, marinating in the sunlight pouring like the sweetest honey from the open windows. The click of high heels on the hardwood drags open my eyes.

Damn.

"Are you going to have brunch with your friends or seduce them?"

Cheeky grin in place, Mai twirls for me. The see-through layers of her dress drift around her hips and thighs before settling like the gossamer wings of a particularly sexy butterfly. She doesn't look like she was nearly stabbed to death less than a week ago.

"Like it?" Mai poses for me, hands on her hips.

"You know I love it."

My woman looks absolutely edible. Her hair is pulled back from her face in tiny braids and twisted into a regal bun at the top of her head. The dress itself barely exists, layered flesh-colored silk that clings to her torso then flares out in an A-line to flutter around her pretty knees. The heels of her emerald-green shoes are high enough to suggest she won't be on her feet much this afternoon.

"Keep everything on when you come to bed tonight. Or maybe just the high heels."

She laughs and drifts over to kiss me very lightly on the mouth. Her expensive matte lipstick is only so smudge-proof, after all. Like a good girl, I keep my hands to myself, although there's nothing more I want to do than drag her down into the sofa with me and kiss her until her clothes fall off.

"I'll see you when I get back," she whispers, gusting her sweet breath over my mouth.

"I'll be right here." My lips capture hers for another brief kiss.

I watch her turn and walk out of the bright living room. "See you later this evening, Ana and Carmen," she calls out toward the kitchen.

My aunts send out a chorus of well-wishes for her afternoon to the soundtrack of Celia Cruz singing out "*Azúcar, azúcar!*"

A coy gaze over her shoulder and Mai is gone. Moments later, I hear the front door open then close.

Even though the tias and I encouraged her to go out and enjoy herself with her friends, she won't be gone long. Since reaffirming our commitment to each other—and being nearly killed by her cousin again—she's stuck close to home. Every night, we make love as if it's our last moment on earth together. Every morning, I wake to her plastered to my side.

Not complaining about that at all.

Everything feels new between us. Our tenderness. Mutual acceptance. Even the condo itself, repaired and refurnished after the Redstones nearly destroyed it.

The thick cushions of the new sofa sigh under my weight as I settle back down to thoughts of what this evening will be like. Mai walking into our bedroom still wearing those heels and her see-through dress. Her smile softened from several drinks and hours of socializing with her friends. I imagine the way she would smile at my nakedness and then—

The doorbell rings.

It's probably Mai. She probably forgot to put her keys into that silly little handbag of hers.

I get up to answer the door. "Did you forget your—" But it's not who I think it is. My jaw clenches. "Mai just left."

"We know."

It's not entirely a surprise to see Mandaia Redstone and Abi on our proverbial doorstep. Whatever their reason for coming here, I'm surprised Cayman's not with them to co-sign his mother's every word. Before my team and I left their house last week, the Redstones been full of worry for Mai. She hadn't wanted to see them, though, not even her sister.

"Please don't shut the door," Abi says quickly when I start to do just that.

My hand clenches around the doorknob. "Like I said before, Mai isn't here. You two can just come back another time since I can't imagine anything you'd have to talk to me about."

"Then you must have a limited imagination."

"Mother!"

But Mandaia Redstone only looks at me with the same implacable expression I've seen on Mai's face a time or two.

"Can we come in?" she asks.

I only debate for a few seconds before waving them inside. After a week of sex, food, and forgiveness, I'm back my full strength. If they pull any shit, I'm more than ready to crush them.

"Would you like something to drink?" Why not be polite?

"Sure," Abi says the same moment that her mother says, "No, thanks. It's not worth the risk of poison."

"Death at my hands wouldn't be as painless as poison," I assure her.

"In that case, I'll have some sparkling water," Mandaia says.

They settle around the small bistro table in the living room while I head to the kitchen and try to be a graceful host. The kitchen is a beautiful wreck of corn husks, dirty dishes, and half-empty margarita glasses.

"Who's out there?" Tia Ana asks, hands on her hips.

When I tell her, she and Tia Carmen give me looks of concern. Tia Ana makes the sign to ward off evil.

"It's fine." Grabbing three bottles of mineral water, I wave off their worry. "They aren't stupid enough to try something after what just happened." At least I hope not. They know I'm an enforcer now, and that means they fear me more than they want to betray me.

Back in the living room, I hand over their water and sit down. "So what can I do for you?" The edge of the sofa sinks beneath my weight.

Mandaia opens her bottle of water and takes a sip. "You're the Absolution Killer." She doesn't say it like a question.

I wait.

Abi is the first to answer my questions. Or at least start to. "We're trying to be better for Mai. She deserves better."

"She doesn't have any problem with you." My gaze moves pointedly to her mother, and I think of the absent Redstones, the father and brother. "The ones who should be making that offer either aren't speaking or aren't here, so I'm not exactly sure about the purpose of being here now with Mai gone."

"Absolution killed people who hurt others." Mandaia's mouth is tight as she speaks.

"Okay. And...?" I'm not giving them a single thing they aren't willing to work for.

"That's why Mom and I thought Absolution wasn't Ethan. He didn't care enough about other people to be any sort of vigilante. His conviction on the basis of him being the Absolution Killer just seemed wrong from the beginning."

"Very astute of you."

"Don't be nasty," Mandaia says, her voice dripping frost.

"Then don't insult my intelligence," I say, equally cold. "Why are you really here?"

In the week since Ethan's death, the case has been laid to rest. Caressa, accused of conspiring with Redstone, was forced to give up her senate seat and now faces the possibility of exile from the family and from the region. Mandaia has reached out to Mai, but my love has been hesitant about extending her hand in return.

"As far as I'm aware, you've never lied to me. That's why I'm here for the truth now," Mandaia toys with the bottle of water, shifting it between each hand. Then she looks directly at me. "Why are you the Absolution Killer? Do the other enforcers know what you've done? Why does Mai accept all this and still love you?"

I have to laugh, thinking about how Mai and I met and where we find ourselves now. "Have you heard of a thing called unconditional love?"

Mandaia Redstone's face is nearly flawless, no hint of the barb that I let fly. But I still see the minute flinch at the edge of her mouth, the tightening of her jaw. And it's only because of these tells that I give her what she asked for.

I tell her and Abi about Ethan killing my sister. About killing Mandaia's brother, Stephen, with my bare hands and enjoying every moment. About how Mai tried to stop me at first, then fell for my irresistible charm.

Abi rolls her eyes but keeps listening. Her mother remains a statue.

Cold and calm, I pour it all out for them, every single thing I know, except for Mai's secrets, until Abi is crying silently in the chair, tears spilling down her cheeks.

"He did something to Mai, didn't he?" Abi clenches her trembling fingers into fists. "That's why Mai didn't want you to go away or be killed for murdering my uncle?"

"That's Mai's story to tell."

With a screech of the chair against the floor, Abi jumps up from the table and runs out of the room. A few seconds later, the door of the powder room slams shut.

"You didn't have to tell her everything." Accusation lays flat and dark in Mandaia's eyes.

"Either you want the truth or you don't. I don't deal in half-lies."

She sighs, and it looks like a painful thing. A gaze flickers toward where Abi has disappeared. "Fair enough." But I see where her fingers dig deep crescents into the edge of the small steel table.

Mai isn't going to like this at all. It's one of the new pieces of furniture we bought to replace what her family destroyed.

"You have the truth, Mandaia." Her name, spoken so casually without the usual caustic bite, feels strange on my tongue. "It's your business what you do with it."

I want truths of my own from Mandaia Redstone. Answers to questions like, who pressured her to help get Ethan free? Did she know what their end game was? But as surely as I have these questions, I know she won't give me the answers.

It's all right, though. I'll dig them up for myself. Later.

Condensation slides down the bottle of water Mandaia hasn't touched in minutes. Her fingers begin smoothing out the marks she made in the table.

"Things have always been difficult with Mai," she says softly, as if talking to herself. "As for my part in all this, I haven't exactly made her struggles any easier." Before I can put enough brain cells together to form an answer, she pushes on. "No one in the family will say a word about your past...hobby as the Absolution Killer. I've spoken with each of them and they know better than to open their mouths about the matter without my permission."

Suspicion raises my hackles. "Do you expect my thanks for that? Some favor I can't refuse?"

"What I *expect*"—she leans hard on the word, eyes flashing a familiar amber fire—"is for you to take care of my daughter."

Mai can take care of herself; that's the real and honest response. But I climb off my asshole high horse for a moment and release a quiet sigh. "I haven't had much success with taking care of the people I love, but I'll do my best with her."

"You love her."

"Of course."

Bracing herself against the table's edge, she gets to her feet. A suddenly old woman. "I'll be in touch."

"Thanks?"

The corner of her mouth twitches into something that might be called a smile on some distant planet. She disappears down the hall to find her younger daughter. When they begin talking, I grab my bottle of still-cold water and lean against the window. The day is still beautiful. Atlanta's mismatch of tall buildings glitters under the sun. Behind me is music and tears, my tias' determined celebration of life, Abi mourning the one Mai escaped from.

Somewhere out there, Mai is laughing. Soon enough, she will come back to me and we'll seek shelter in each other's smiles. We'll share the massive batch of tamales with my tias, and the trust, the acceptance, between all four of us will continue to grow.

It's more than I deserve, but I plan to hold tight to this happiness.

The bottle of mineral water hisses when I twist off the cap. Cool on my tongue, the water washes down my throat like a cleansing. A sensation of renewal. It feels good.

CHAPTER 27

"Hey, what's wrong?"

Mai appears in the doorway of our living room, a mirror of when she left earlier. Like in my fantasies from this afternoon, she is loose and beautiful after spending the day with her friends and good liquor. Sunset hovers more than an hour away, and the softer colors of the late afternoon bleed through the sheer curtains and suffuse Mai's skin.

My heart trips from just looking at her.

Sitting up in the couch, I put aside the book I was reading. "Your mother and sister came for a visit while you were gone."

I keep my voice low, aware of my tias quietly talking and playing Scrabble in the guest room.

A gasp of concern and apology. Mai rushes to my side and drops to her knees in front of me. Her eyes desperately look me over. "What happened? Did my mother hurt you?"

"No." I nearly scoff, but then I remember not so long ago and in this actual apartment, that's exactly what happened. "She wanted to ask me some questions. I gave her the answers. She should be calling you at some point."

Mai drops her head in my lap, hands convulsively clasp my thighs. "She already did. About an hour ago." Her fingers are trembling and cold. "I just...don't know what to make of her lunch invitation."

That was fast. "You should accept it."

"Really?" She looks up at me, her eyes wide in surprise. "What... what changed your mind?"

"You love your family. You need them." It's a truth neither of us can escape. "Your mother is asking your forgiveness and ready to do what she can to make you happy."

"Her not trying to kill you would make me happy."

"Then we're already there. She and Abi came by and left everything in one piece, including me." I lean down and press a kiss to her unsmiling mouth. "That should make you practically dance on the ceiling."

"This isn't a Lionel Richie video, Xóchitl."

I huff a laugh and trail my fingers along the tiny braids above her hair. "You kn—"

That particular ring of Mai's cell phone cuts me off.

"Uh-oh." I release her with a reluctant sigh. "You're being summoned."

"It's not like that," Mai says, already moving away from me. Her high heels clatter to the floor along with my fantasies about how the rest of the night would end. "I'll be back as soon as I can."

"I know." Her stilletos clack together when I scoop them up from the floor and follow her to the bedroom.

"It's me," she says into the phone while tugging off her pretty dress. She throws it on the bed with a regretful look in my direction. "Got it. I'm on the way now."

She ends the call and tosses the phone next to the dress, already Mercy in head-to-toe oxblood leather, her skin supple yet hard enough to stop bullets. She's another of my fantasies come to life.

"Bad traffic accident."

"Can't they handle that on their own?"

"Don't be a baby." And with that, she is gone, slipping through the window like smoke.

"She's as bad as you." My Tia Ana comes from the direction of the guest room on silent feet. "Always wanting to save the world."

"I don't want to save the world, Tia. I just want to kick its ass—huge difference."

"Whatever you say, love. Just be careful out there."

"What do you mean?" I ask, not sure why I even bother trying to fool her.

"Go on." With a knowing laugh, she waves a hand at me and heads back toward the room. "We'll make sure you two have a nice, healthy breakfast in the morning."

Not wasting any more time, I slip on a new outfit bought especially for a night like this one and head out after Mai.

They were right to call her. It's not just an accident; it's a disaster.

A highway overpass cracked in two. Cars on both ends of the missing ten-foot section crumpled together. People screaming and crying. A few douchebags taking video with their cell phones instead of trying to help or even getting out of the way.

Underneath the overpass, thirty feet below, the missing section lays in pieces. It's crushed cars, people.

God damn…

As if all that isn't bad enough, a tractor-trailer hangs half on, half off the broken lip of the overpass, its two front wheels hanging in thin air. The cab of the truck points down to the steep drop below. There are cars everywhere.

Why is there bumper-to-bumper traffic in Atlanta at seven o'clock on a Sunday evening? Because it's Atlanta, that's why.

The tractor-trailer groans and see-saws from the edge of the broken overpass. Movement behind the steering wheel catches my eye.

Seriously?

The driver is still in the truck and trying to crawl into the back and away from the drop that would kill him and anyone still left in the cars just below. It's a shit show, and I'm not sure if they can get out of this without any more people dying.

"What's the status?" I hear Mai ask one of the cops.

But it's obvious enough. Everything's fucked up. Looks like some kind of explosive went off and took out part of the highway. The flaming remnants of a car exhales dark clouds of smoke from underneath the hanging truck. Other cars have already fallen into the jagged gap of concrete, crushed and warped from the impact. People nearby scream for rescue and crawl from vehicles in danger of going up in flames.

The cops are here. Ambulances and fire trucks, too, all with their sirens and lights blazing. Even more emergency vehicles are coming, but it's much more than they can handle.

"I'll do what I can," she shouts as I take in the chaos through her eyes. Then she rushes in to get at the big, dangling problem first.

"Mercy!" a woman screams from one of the flaming cars. Her feeling of relief at seeing Mai comes at me like a massive wave.

Are these people stupid? Don't they get it? Mai alone isn't enough to get them out of this mess.

Shit.

Already regretting my foolishness, I leap from the top of a car where I've been watching and drop down between the crack in the overpass and down, down to the road below. Scorched air and smoke rush over my face.

The smell of melted plastics, cooking human flesh, and burnt paint chokes me. My foot splashes in a puddle of blood as I run to the first car.

At the steering wheel, a woman slumps over unconscious, blood flowing from the gash in her head. Something inside the car is hot and blowing smoke.

"Help her! Please!"

A man tries to yank open the car door and get to her. Pieces of broken glass dig into his hand as he frantically pulls at the door. With one arm hanging loose and bloody at his side, he looks ready to pass out, too.

"Please, help! I don't know what to do!"

I rip the car door off its hinges and toss it aside, then handle the stuck seatbelt the same way. Carefully, I lift the woman out of the car. She's barely any weight at all.

"Come on! Follow me." With the limp woman in my arms, I race from the smoking car, making sure her man is keeping up with me, or at least enough not to get roasted when the car blows up.

Suddenly, the car does just that. I drag the man in front of me so anything flying from the exploding car hits me and not him or the woman in my arms. A breath of heated air licks over my back, but I don't stop running.

Once we're a safe enough distance away from the flames and chaos, I prop the woman on a concrete pylon and push the man down next to her.

"The ambulance is coming. Stay here." Then I leave them to find more.

As fast as possible, I grab people from their cars and pull them to safety, tucking them away from the flames and deadly fumes while keeping part of my attention on Mai and the truck she's trying to keep from falling into the chasm.

Babies. Old people. Teenagers. A set of twins on the way home from some kind of sporting game.

I hear the creak of the tractor-trailer. Feel Mai cool and calm, grabbing the driver out of the swaying truck cab, balancing carefully so he won't fall and she doesn't, either. She has him and is taking him away from the truck, nimbly running away from the see-sawing vehicle.

"It's falling!" a man screams.

Yep. That's definitely what it's doing.

A quick scan of the minds I can feel confirms there's no one else under here in danger of being crushed by the truck. But the truck's fall won't be such a pretty thing, either. Mai is busy. She has the driver safely in the arms of a paramedic and is about to rush back to the truck when it lets out a dying screech.

A chorus of screams rises up.

I rush out into the open and look up in time to see the truck cab tip over the open edge of the highway crack and nosedive toward me and the other cars down here. *Shit. It's still hooked to the trailer.*

A loud cry. A child. I suddenly feel it, a mind that I missed before. The young boy must have been passed out when I did my last mental scan of the area.

How many others did I miss?

I curse again and quickly scan the area looking for another option other than the stupid one running through my head.

It's not stupid, it's crazy, but it's just crazy enough to work. Mai's voice comes through loud and clear in my head.

I don't have time to be surprised. The truck is falling and people are terrified, scrambling away from the howling weight of the semi.

Without the humans around, this decision would be an easy one to make, but things are what they are.

Let's do it, Mai!

The truck's fall and the decision to save it feel like they take forever, but it's barely a second.

Mai jumps off the overpass. Screams of warning and wonder rise as her body flies into the air and down toward the falling truck. It's a long way down, and none of the humans know what the hell she's trying to pull. I know what she's doing and even I don't have much faith in it.

A beat later, her tail whips out and wraps around the railing. She grabs the back of the trailer, hands crunching into the steel the same moment I leap up, high and hard, grabbing the cab.

The truck bends where the cab connects to the full trailer. Motor oil bursts from the truck and splashes in my face, hot and viscous. At least the back of the trailer isn't open.

Carefully controlling the awkward weight of the semi, I float-fall back down as slowly as possible with gravity threatening to drag me down hard the whole way. Motor oil slides down my face and into my mouth. I spit and try not to gag.

Above me, Mai's tail slowly lengthens and unwinds like a winch, giving her the space to move down as slowly as the truck's descent will allow. Together, we lower the truck to the ground. It lands with a hard, ground-shaking thump, crushes a string of empty cars.

Wide-eyed, Mai releases her end of the truck and lets go of the overpass railing with her tail.

Damn, it worked.

A rush of amazement comes from the humans, but hell if it doesn't also feel like my own.

"Okay."

With the truck safely on the ground to the wild applause going on, she walks around the ruins of the burning cars and comes up to me. Dirt streaks her face. Her breath comes in deep gasps.

"Thanks for helping," she says.

"I couldn't let you do all the work."

She laughs, and it sounds like relief. "Can't you just say 'you're welcome' like a normal person?"

"How boring would that be?"

Mai's smile is small but radiant. "Thanks for stepping in. I know you like to watch but having you in the thick of things is nice."

Wait. "You knew I was following you?"

"Sure. Maybe not from the beginning, but you're not as subtle as you think."

A flush of embarrassment threats to catch my face on fire. "I need to work on that."

"Not really." Her voice is as gentle as the unexpected touch of her fingers in the small of my back. "I like that you're an open book to me. Mostly open, anyway."

Sirens shriek between here and the hospital a few miles away. Bright lights flash blue and red against the background of night. Around us, people rush and news helicopters circle. It's late. Past midnight at least.

With the worst of it done, people are suddenly interested in us, in me. I feel their thoughts. And through their eyes, I see us, or at least I see me. Dressed all in black with my face covered, an exact shadow replica of Mai.

Time to get out of here. "See you at home."

Mai will probably stay and help with the cleanup.

She grabs my arm. "Thank you for following me. Thank you for loving me."

"Please, don't..." My tongue swipes over my dry lips. "It's impossible for me to do anything else."

A hint of a smile briefly shapes her mouth. "And that's just one of the reasons I love you so much."

Her words implode inside me. Shudders of gladness ripple up my spine, down my arms, through my entire body. "Yeah?"

Although I knew how she felt, this is the first time the words have left her lips.

"Yeah," she confirms with that same tiny smile.

My laugh bursts out. "That's...okay."

Then, because I'm about to start grinning like a fool, I leave.

I take off in the opposite direction from the mob of reporters. Soon, I'm back at the house, slipping into the window and then stripping off my clothes in the bathroom.

She loves me.

My laughter is soft and private in the shower-steamed bathroom. I can definitely live with that.

As I step, smiling, under the heated spray of the shower, the bathroom door opens then closes. The shower is glassed in, but there's a wall hiding my view of the actual bathroom door.

It can only be one person.

"Mai?" I call out anyway.

"Who else do you expect to follow you home and get into the bathroom with you?"

The teasing note in her words makes me smile. "I thought you were going to stay a little longer."

"I'm needed here more," she says, her voice coming closer.

"Why? Because you weakened me with your declaration of love and want to make sure I've survived the aftermath?" The smile makes my cheeks ache but I wear it the whole time I scrub myself raw with my washcloth and tangerine-scented soap.

"No, I'm pretty sure you can handle that." She pauses, her delicate footsteps sounding gently against the tile floors. "You...you know this hero thing isn't what I expect you to do, right?" Mai steps into view wearing shorts and a tank top and sits down on the padded bench seat across from the shower. The seriousness of her words pushes away my smile. "You don't have to save people because that's what I choose to do. This isn't a condition of me being with you."

"I know." Bubbles slide from my skin and circle the drain.

Mai's low sigh comes softly. "Before, I was angry that you chose not to use your gifts the way I do. That's not fair. I can admit that now. All I want is for you to be you and for us to be together."

My heart thumps wildly. All I can do is stand still under the hot spray, water running over my head and into my eyes.

"I-I appreciate that." Despite the water rushing over me, my lips feel dry.

I lick them and turn away from the open expression that sits so effortlessly on her face. Although we've talked about what it means for us to be together since that craziness with Ethan last week, this is the first time she's actually apologized for wanting me to be other than I am.

"That doesn't seem like that much to ask." I tease her with the return of my smile.

"Good." She breathes out a sigh, a matching smile curving up her mouth. "Now hurry up. Ana and Carmen have breakfast waiting and you don't want it to get cold."

It's way too early for breakfast, but I don't want to rain on their parade.

She stands up and puts her palm against the shower glass. I press my cheek to the warmth seeping through the glass from her skin and into me. "I'll be right there."

"And I'll be waiting," she says softly.

We share a long look before she turns and leaves me under the water, breathing easily for the first time in weeks.

ABOUT FIONA ZEDDE

Jamaican-born Fiona Zedde currently lives and writes in Atlanta, Georgia. She is the author of several novellas and novels of lesbian love and desire, including the Lambda Literary Award finalists, *Bliss* and *Every Dark Desire*. Her novel, *Dangerous Pleasures*, was winner of the About.com Readers' Choice Award for Best Lesbian Novel or Memoir of 2012.

Her short fiction has appeared in various anthologies including the Cleis Press Best Lesbian Erotica series, *Wicked: Sexy Tales of Legendary Lovers*, *Iridescence: Sensuous Shades of Lesbian Erotica*, and *Fist of the Spider Woman*.

CONNECT WITH FIONA
Website: www.fionazedde.com
E-Mail: f.zedde@gmail.com

OTHER BOOKS FROM YLVA PUBLISHING

www.ylva-publishing.com

SHATTERED

The Superheroines Collection
Lee Winter

ISBN: 978-3-95533-563-2
Length: 194 pages (69,000 words)

Shattergirl, Earth's first lesbian guardian is refusing to save people and has gone off the grid. Lena Martin, the street-smart tracker with a silver tongue and a disdain for the rogue guardians she chases, has only days to bring her home. As the pair clash heatedly, masks begin to crack and brutal secrets are exposed that could shatter them both.

THE POWER OF MERCY

The Superheroines Collection
Fiona Zedde

ISBN: 978-3-95533-854-1
Length: 113 pages (37,000 words)

To her family, Mai Redstone is weak. When she becomes Mercy, a rooftop-climbing chameleon with at least nine lives, she finds her power. But when Mercy is called in by police to a murder case, her whole world threatens to crumble. The dead man made her childhood a hell. She is torn between giving the murderer a medal and finding the killer for her family. Mercy is a blade that can cut both ways.

CHASING STARS

The Superheroines Collection

Alex K. Thorne

ISBN: 978-3-95533-992-0

Length: 205 pages (70,000 words)

For superhero Swiftwing, crime fighting isn't her biggest battle. Nor is it having to meet the whims of Hollywood star Gwen Knight as her mild-mannered assistant, Ava. It's doing all that, while tracking a giant alien bug, being asked to fake date her famous boss, and realizing that she might be coming down with a pesky case of feelings.

A fun, sweet, sexy lesbian romance about the masks we wear.

SHADOW HAND

The Superheroines Collection

Sacchi Green

ISBN: 978-3-96324-109-3

Length: 232 pages (77,000 words)

A long-buried stone goddess bestows on US Army Lt. Ashton the power to move objects with her mind. Ash seeks a way to use her ability, while avoiding any outside forces—military or mythical. She also must find a way to control it, before it controls her. Ash turns to her tough, steadfast lover Cleo, who has special skills of her own, to help in the struggle. Can Cleo keep Ash rooted in humanity?

ISBN: 978-3-96324-206-9

Also available as e-book.

Published by Ylva Publishing, legal entity of Ylva Verlag, e.Kfr.

Ylva Verlag, e.Kfr.
Owner: Astrid Ohletz
Am Kirschgarten 2
65830 Kriftel
Germany

www.ylva-publishing.com

First edition: 2019

Credits
Edited by Lee Winter and Amanda Jean
Cover Design and Print Layout by Streetlight Graphics

www.ingramcontent.com/pod-product-compliance
Lightning Source LLC
Chambersburg PA
CBHW031145050726
47495CB00018B/1149